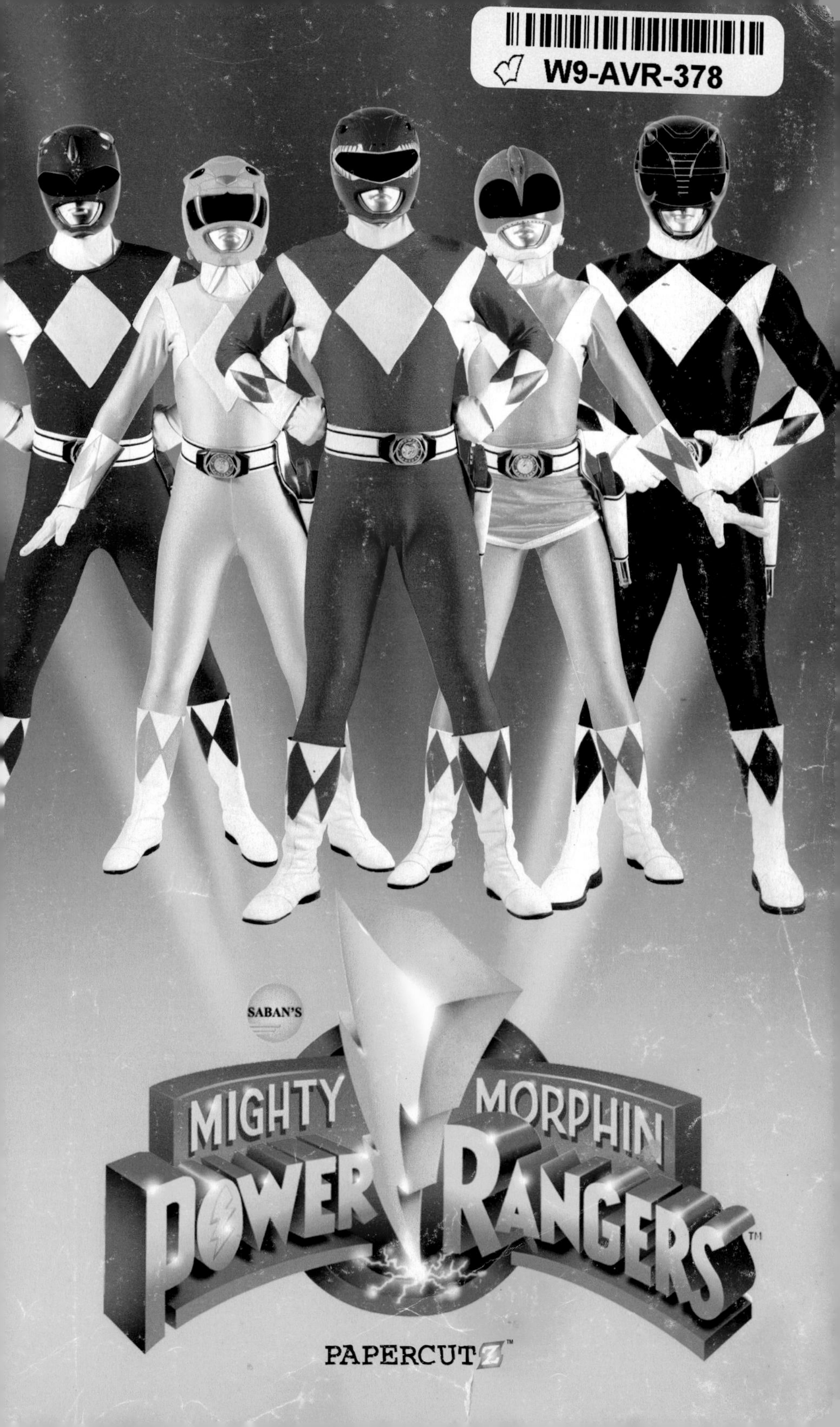

SABAN'S

# MIGHTY MORPHIN POWER RANGERS™

PAPERCUTZ™

# Graphic Novels Available from Papercutz

# MIGHTY MORPHIN POWER RANGERS™

SABAN'S

## ➋ "GOING GREEN"

**Stefan Petrucha & Ryan Buell** – Writers

**PH Marcondes** – Artist

**Mindy Indy** – Colorist

PAPERCUTZ™

MIGHTY MORPHIN POWER RANGERS #2
"Going Green"

STEFAN PETRUCHA & RYAN BUELL – Writers
PH MARCONDES – Artist
MINDY INDY – Colorist
BRYAN SENKA – Letterer

UMESH PATEL (RANGER CREW) – Special Thanks
KAY OLIVER, MARY RAFFERTY, EDGAR PASTEN, GREG SANTOS, VICKI JAEGER – Extra Special Thanks
ALEXANDER LU – Editorial Intern
BETH SCORZATO – Production Coordinator
MICHAEL PETRANEK – Editor
JIM SALICRUP
Editor-in-Chief

ISBN: 978-1-62991-051-2 paperback edition
ISBN: 978-1-62991-052-9 hardcover edition

Printed in China
November 2014 by WKT CO. LTD
3/F Phase I Leader Industrial Centre
188 Texaco Road, Tseun Wan, Hong Kong

Papercutz books may be purchased for business or promotional use. For information on bulk purchases please contact
Macmillan Corporate and Premium Sales Department at (800) 221-7945 x5442.

Distributed by Macmillan

First Printing

MIGHTY MORPHIN **Power Rangers**™

After 10,000 years of imprisonment, the evil sorceress Rita Repulsa and her loyal minions were freed from their space dumpster, when astronauts on a routine mission accidentally opened it on the moon. Enraged, Rita decided to conquer the nearest planet-- Earth. But her arch nemesis, the heroic sage Zordon, had been patiently waiting for this day.

Zordon recruited 5 "teenagers with attitude"-- Jason, Kimberly, Billy, Trini, and Zack-- banded together as the Mighty Morphin Power Rangers and repeatedly defeated Rita. In response, Rita has decided to adopt a new method for conquering Earth and destroying the Power Rangers: creating an evil ranger of her own. Her candidate? Tommy Oliver...

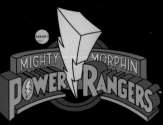

# THE RED RANGER (JASON LEE SCOTT)

Jason is a black belt in karate and the leader of the Power Rangers. His martial arts are his passion and he spends much of his free time training, both learning new moves and perfecting old ones. When he's not training, Jason is working on his schoolwork or hanging out with friends like most other seventeen-year-old guys.

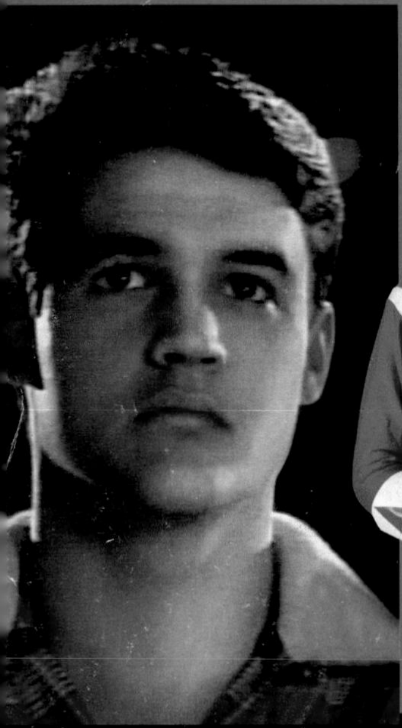

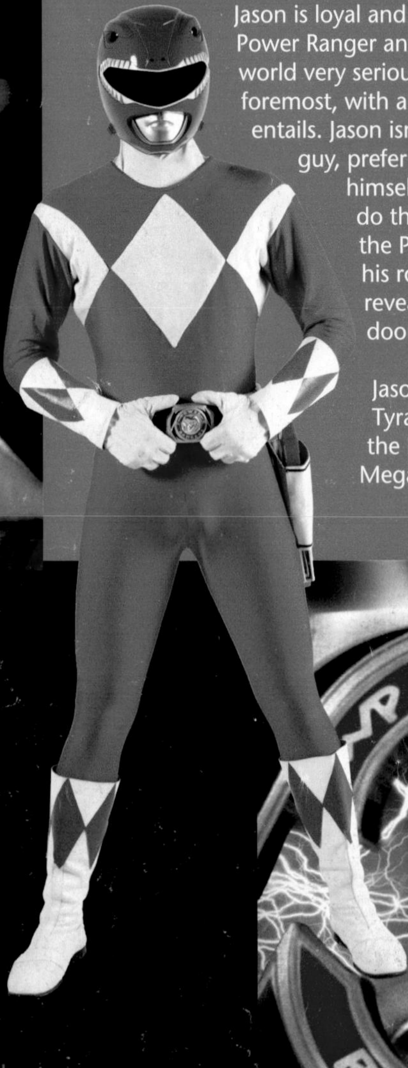

Jason is loyal and patriotic. He loves being a Power Ranger and takes his duty to save the world very seriously. But he's still a teen first ar foremost, with all the trials and tribulations th entails. Jason isn't always the most outspoker guy, preferring to keep his feelings to himself, and letting his hands and fe do the talking while fighting with the Power Rangers. But even with his rough exterior, his sly smile car reveal the mischievous boy-next-door he is at heart.

Jason draws power from the Tyrannosaurus rex. His weapon is the Power Sword, and he pilots th Megazord when it is fully assemble

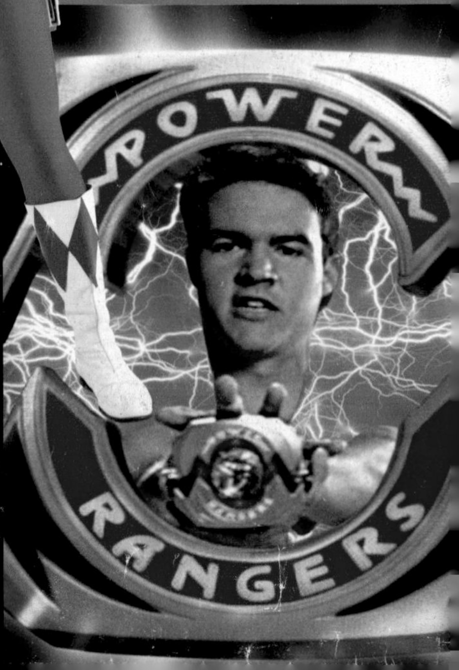
POWER
RANGERS

**Weapon:**
Power Sword

**Zord:**
Tyrannosaurus Dinozord

**Notes:**
Jason was a martial arts instructor at Ernie's Juice Bar and Gym.

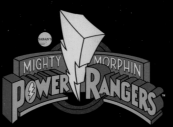

# THE PINK RANGER (KIMBERLY HART)

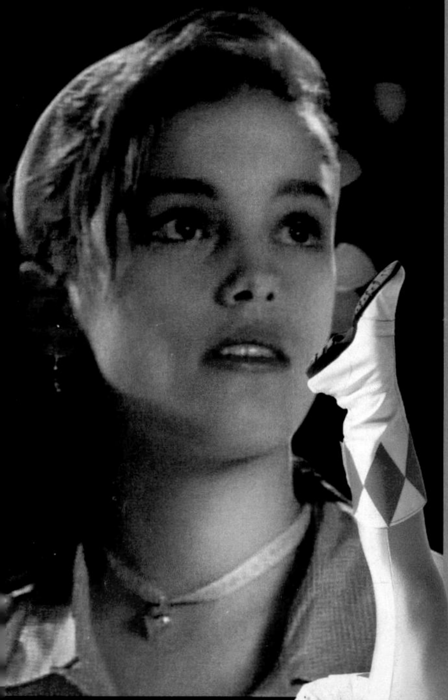

Kimberly is a bright and beautiful girl who loves shopping and gymnastics. She's the most popular girl at school and loves being in the limelight. But beneath her bubbly exterior she's fiercely independent and has always longed for adventure and danger. Kimberly is always upbeat with her friends, but she's got a wicked streak of sarcasm and one-liners that she saves for the bad guys.

Kimberly is also a champion gymnast, and she brings these skills to her work with the Power Rangers. She trains hard not just to compete, but also to be able to jump and flip her way out of almost any situation. With the Power Rangers, Kimberly draws power from the Pterodactyl and her weapon is the Power Bow.

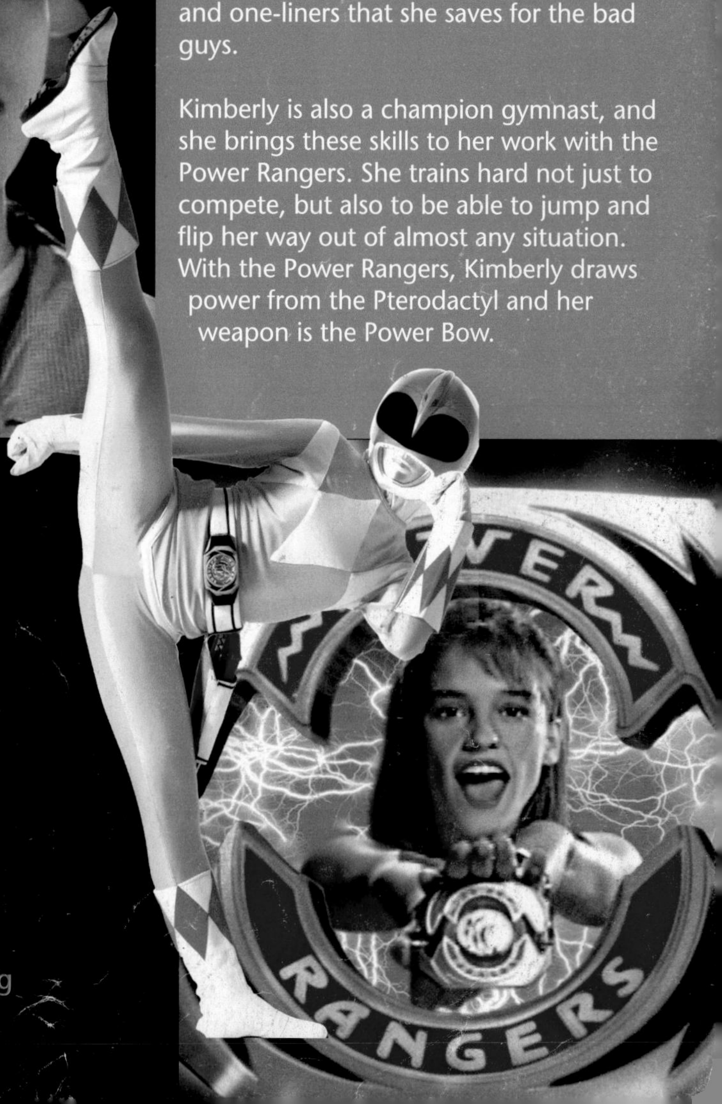
POWER
RANGERS

**eapon:**
ower Bow

**rd:**
terodactyl
Dinozord

**tes:**
ocal bully Skull has a big
rush on her.

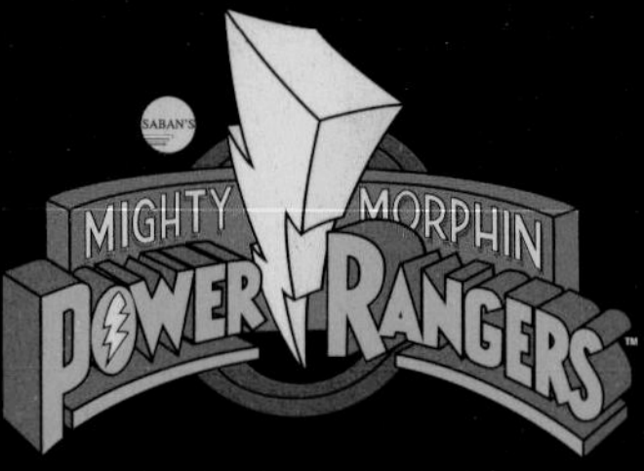

# THE BLUE RANGER (BILLY CRANSTON)

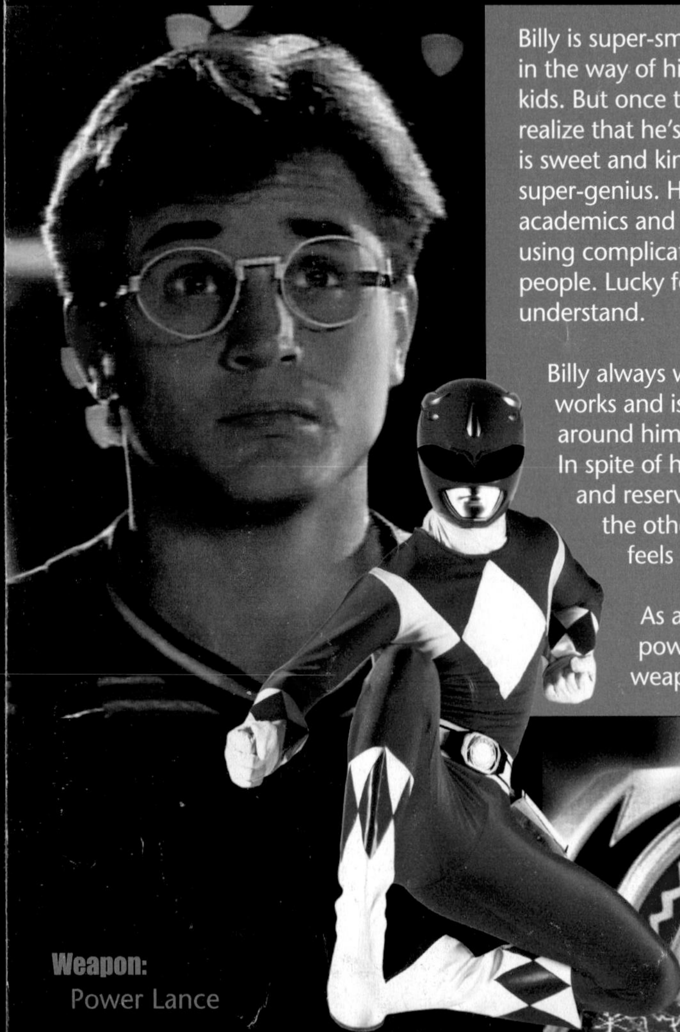

Billy is super-smart and this can sometimes get in the way of him communicating with other kids. But once they get to know him, they realize that he's more than just a nerd. Billy is sweet and kind-hearted, on top of being a super-genius. He focuses all his energy on his academics and often talks in techno-speak, using complicated language that confuses mos people. Lucky for him, Trini always seems to understand.

Billy always wants to know how everything works and is constantly studying the world around him. His greatest hobby is learning In spite of his intelligence, Billy is usually sh and reserved, except for with his friends, the other Power Rangers. With them h feels like he can truly be himself.

As a Power Ranger, Billy draws power from the Triceratops and his weapon is the Power Lance.

**Weapon:**
Power Lance

**Zord:**
Triceratops
Dinozord

**Notes:**
Billy built the Power Ranger communicators.

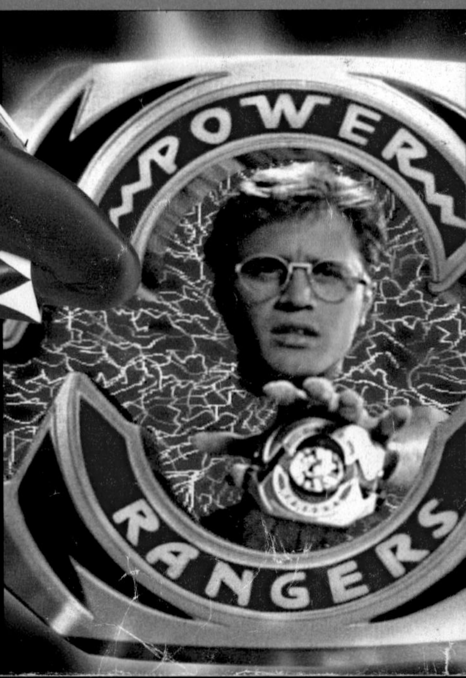
POWER
RANGERS

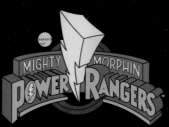

# THE YELLOW RANGER (TRINI KWAN)

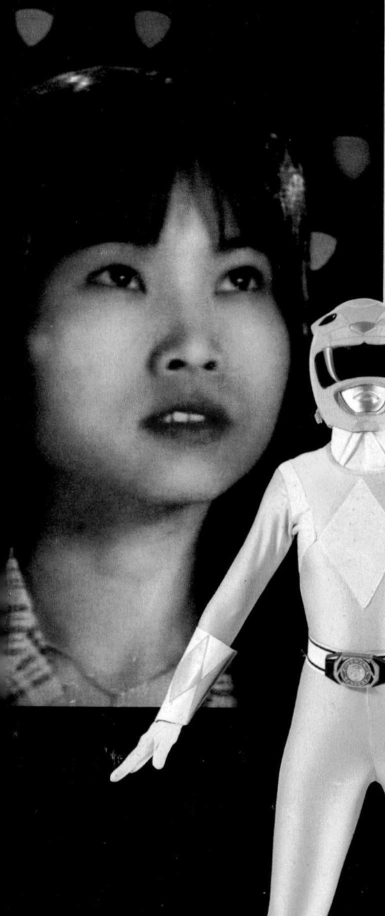

Trini has been described by Zordon himself as the one with "lightning hands and a peaceful soul." She is deeply dedicated to her martial arts practice, constantly working on both the spiritual and physical aspects of her karate. Trini is highly observant and highly intelligent, which makes her the only person who truly understands Billy. At school, Trini is active in lots of activities and causes and is a role model for other students.

Even with her extraordinary gifts, she is very patient and slow to anger. But, if pushed, she will shut down any threat with little effort. When her training takes over, she is a razor-sharp fighter with lightning reflexes.

With the Power Rangers, Trini draws power from the Sabertooth Tiger, and her weapon is the Power Daggers.

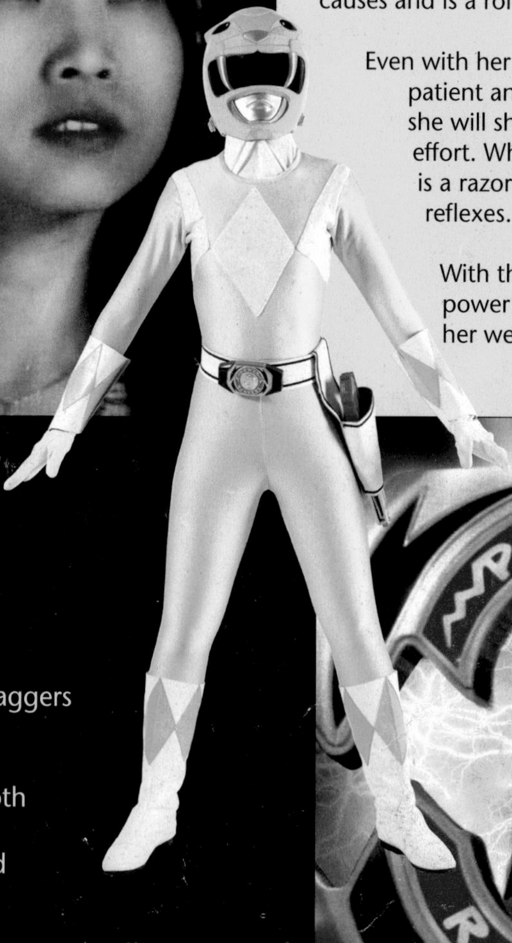

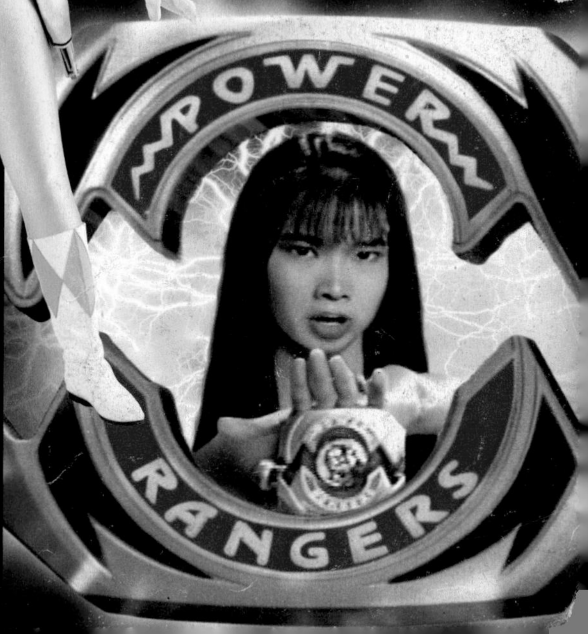
POWER
RANGERS

**eapon:**
ower Daggers

**rd:**
Sabertooth
Tiger
Dinozord

**tes:**
rini has a secret fear of heights.

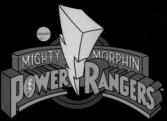

# THE BLACK RANGER (ZACK TAYLOR)

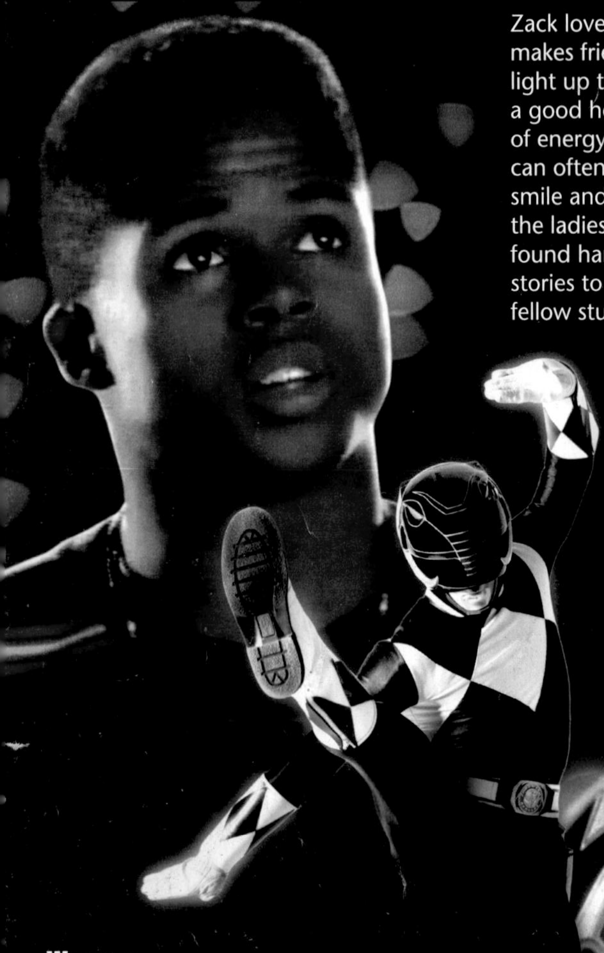

Zack loves life and always lives to the fullest. He makes friends with everyone and can always light up the room with his personality. He's got a good heart and a seemingly boundless supply of energy. Smooth talking and street-smart, he can often disarm his opponents with a quick smile and his wit. He also fancies himself quite the ladies' man. At school, Zack can often be found hanging around the music rooms, telling stories to a crowd in the quad, or helping out a fellow student.

Zack is intelligent and offers a good balance to Jason's often gung-ho style. Though he's very courageous, he will also often act as the voice of caution in unclear situations. Intuition is Zack's guide and he'll often act based on hunches and instincts.

As a Power Ranger, Zack draws his power from the Mastadon and his weapon is the Power Axe.

**Weapon:**
Power Axe

**Zord:**
Mastodon
Dinozord

**Notes:**
Zack developed his own special fighting style: Hip Hop Kido.

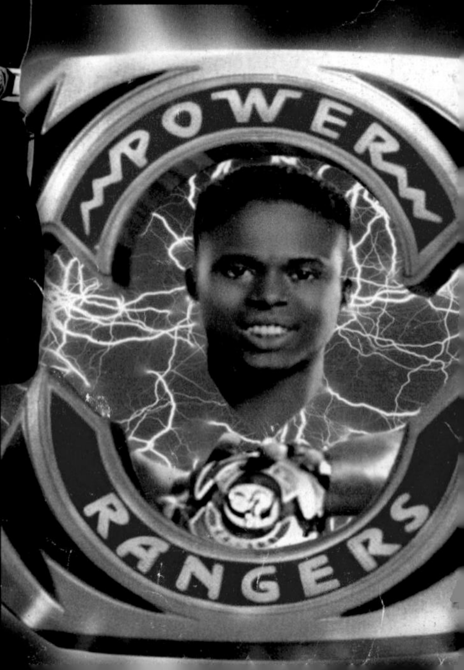
POWER
RANGERS

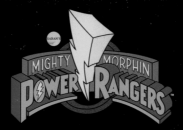

SABAN'S MIGHTY MORPHIN POWER RANGERS™

# TOMMY OLIVER

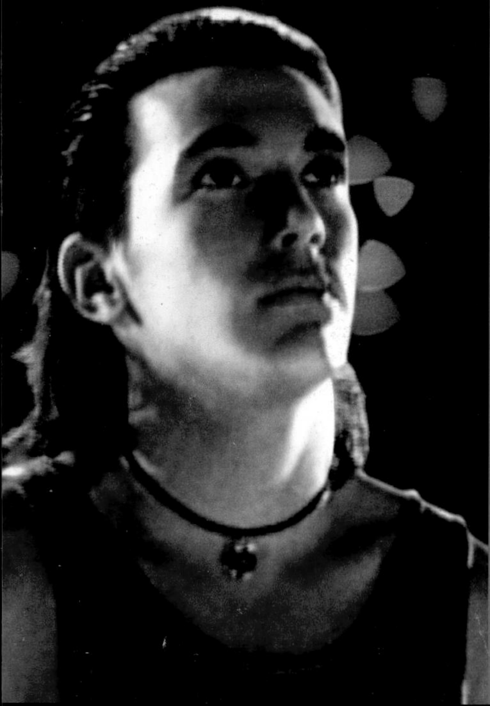

Tommy Oliver is new to Angel Grove, having just moved to the area with his family. He is a Freshman at Angel Grove High School. Little is known about Tommy's past except that he is an orphan, and was adopted by the Oliver family at a very young age.

An expert in Karate, Tommy took an interest in martial arts at a young age, excelling in amateur competitions. He looks to continue practicing his love of martial arts, which brings him to a studio in Angel Grove where another expert martial artist is said to practice-- Jason Lee Scott.

Tommy Oliver will become the greatest of Power Rangers someday, but today he is just a normal teen with extraordinary fighting abilities looking to start fresh in a new city. The future holds a destiny for Tommy Olver that will lead to a life beyond his wildest dreams.

**eapon:**
Quick thinking and reflexes.

**rd:**
None. For now...

**tes:**
ommy is one of the only humans vithout superpowers capable of vining in hand-to-hand combat gainst Rita Repulsa's putty patrol.

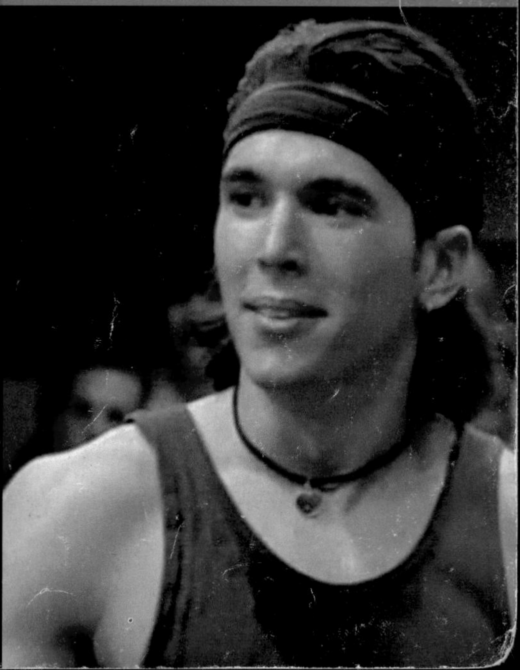

# ZORDON AND ALPHA 5

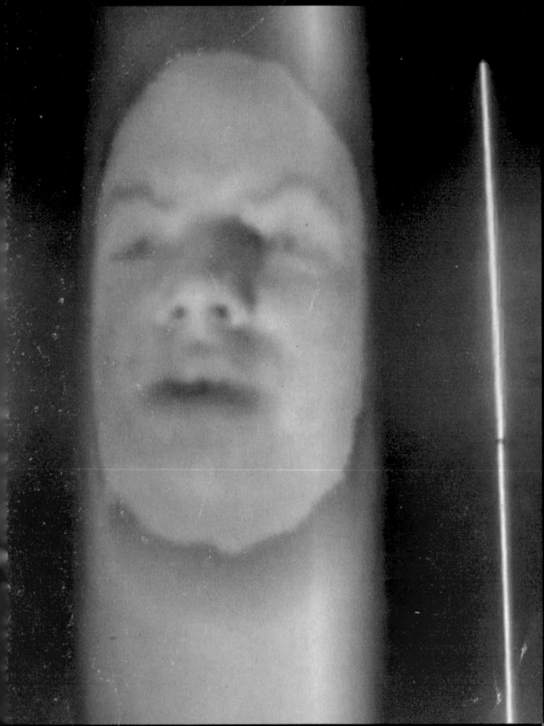

Zordon is a wise, kind, and ageless galactic sage who has always fought for the side of good against evil, and created the Power Rangers. Trapped in an interdimensional time warp, his only way of communicating is through a holographic device built by Alpha 5 in the Command Center. From the he monitors Rita's actions, and directs the Power Rangers in their missions

Zordon has fought Rita Repulsa and her factions over thousands of years. Knowing that she might one day return to continue her war on Earth, Zordon built a base know as the Command Center, where he recruite the Power Rangers.

Alpha 5 is a robot in the service of Zordon who has been at his side since the beginnin of time. He cares for Zordon and the Powe Rangers, constantly keeping them on targe with his reminders of the tasks at hand.

**Weapon:**
  Intelligence, creativity.

**Zord:**
  None.

**Notes:**
  Zordon hid key weapons across the universe in anticipation of the return of evil.

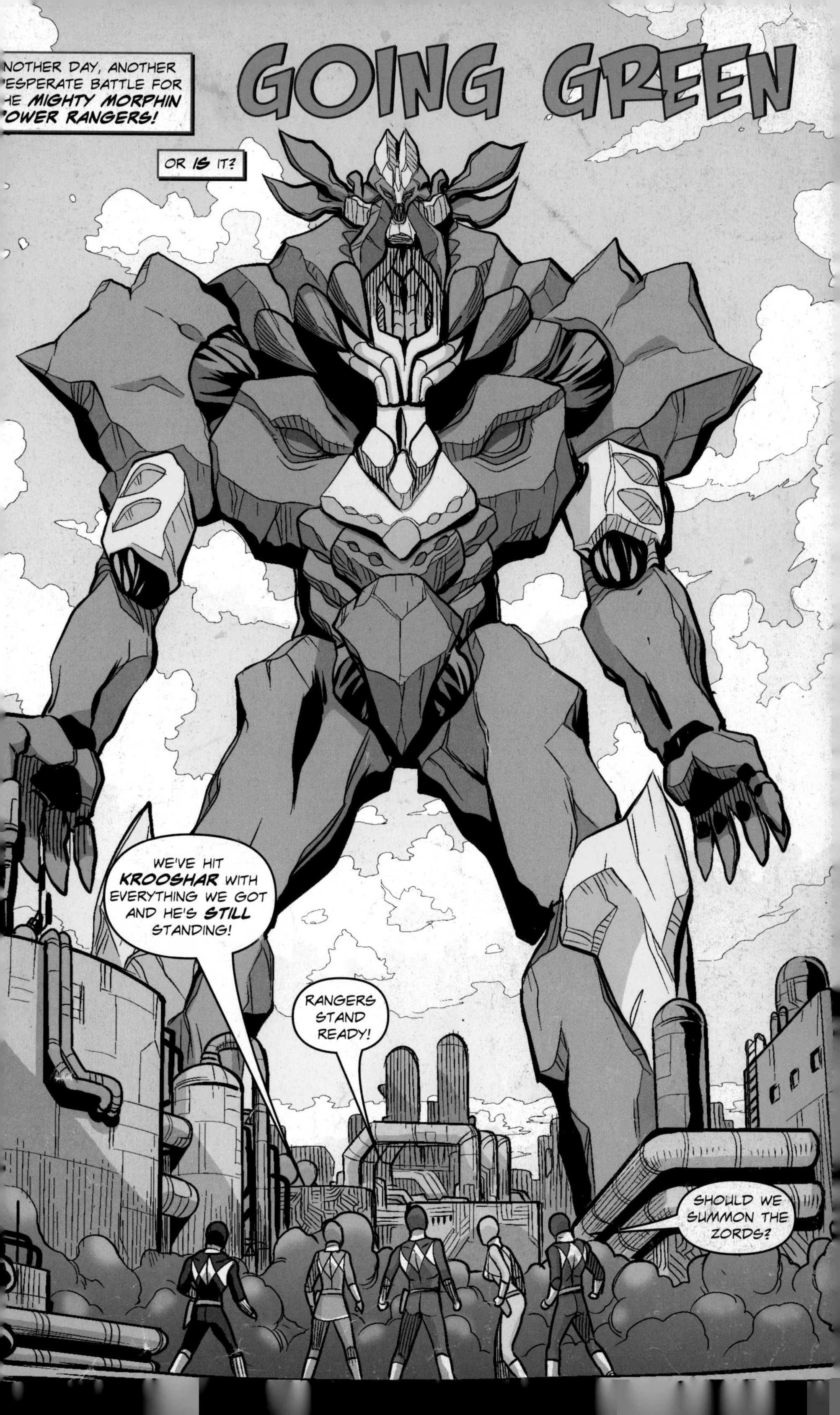
NOTHER DAY, ANOTHER ESPERATE BATTLE FOR HE MIGHTY MORPHIN OWER RANGERS!
GOING GREEN
OR IS IT?
WE'VE HIT KROOSHAR WITH EVERYTHING WE GOT AND HE'S STILL STANDING!
RANGERS STAND READY!
SHOULD WE SUMMON THE ZORDS?

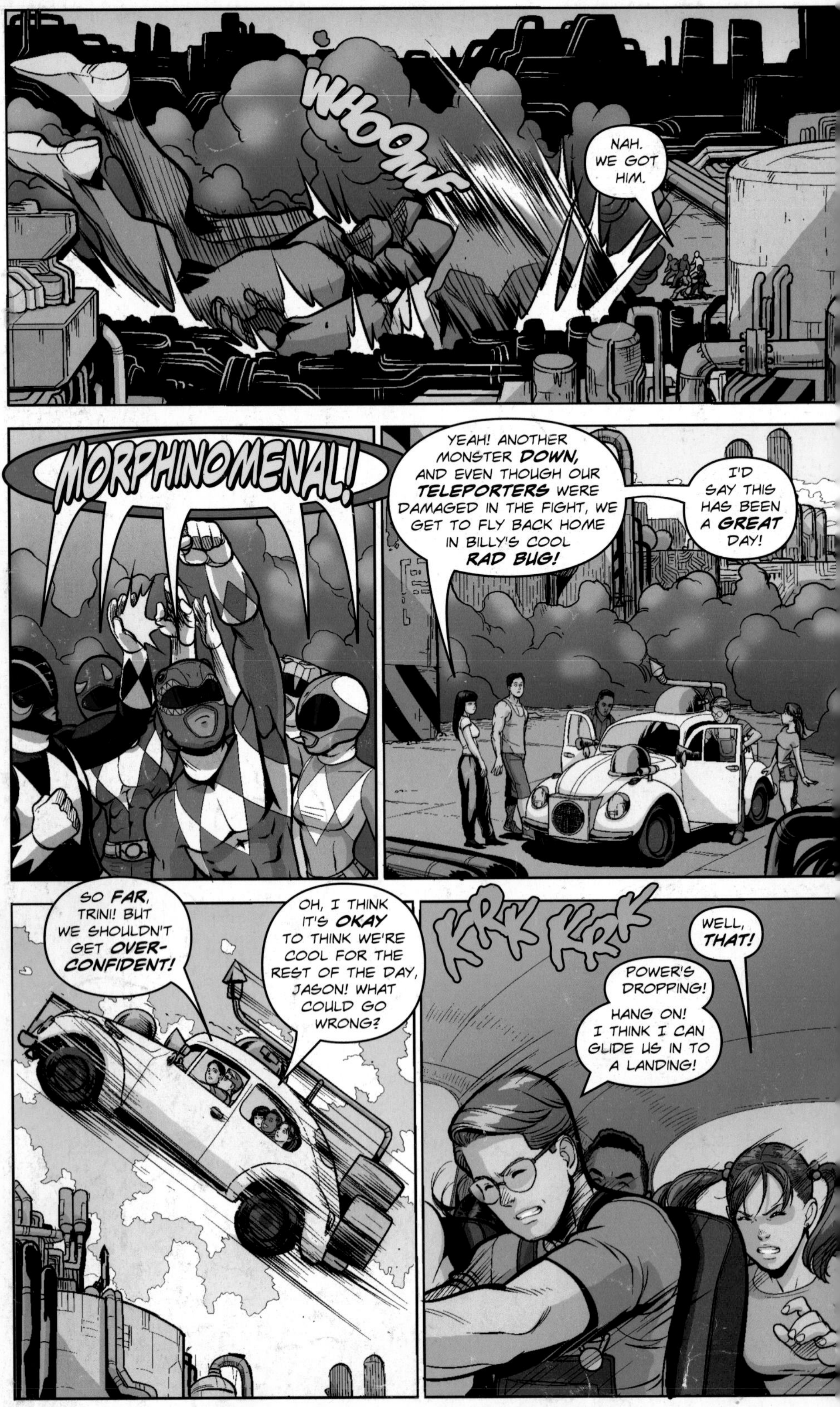
WHOOMF
NAH. WE GOT HIM.
MORPHINOMENAL!
YEAH! ANOTHER MONSTER DOWN, AND EVEN THOUGH OUR TELEPORTERS WERE DAMAGED IN THE FIGHT, WE GET TO FLY BACK HOME IN BILLY'S COOL RAD BUG!
I'D SAY THIS HAS BEEN A GREAT DAY!
SO FAR, TRINI! BUT WE SHOULDN'T GET OVER-CONFIDENT!
OH, I THINK IT'S OKAY TO THINK WE'RE COOL FOR THE REST OF THE DAY, JASON! WHAT COULD GO WRONG?
KRK KRK
WELL, THAT!
POWER'S DROPPING!
HANG ON! I THINK I CAN GLIDE US IN TO A LANDING!

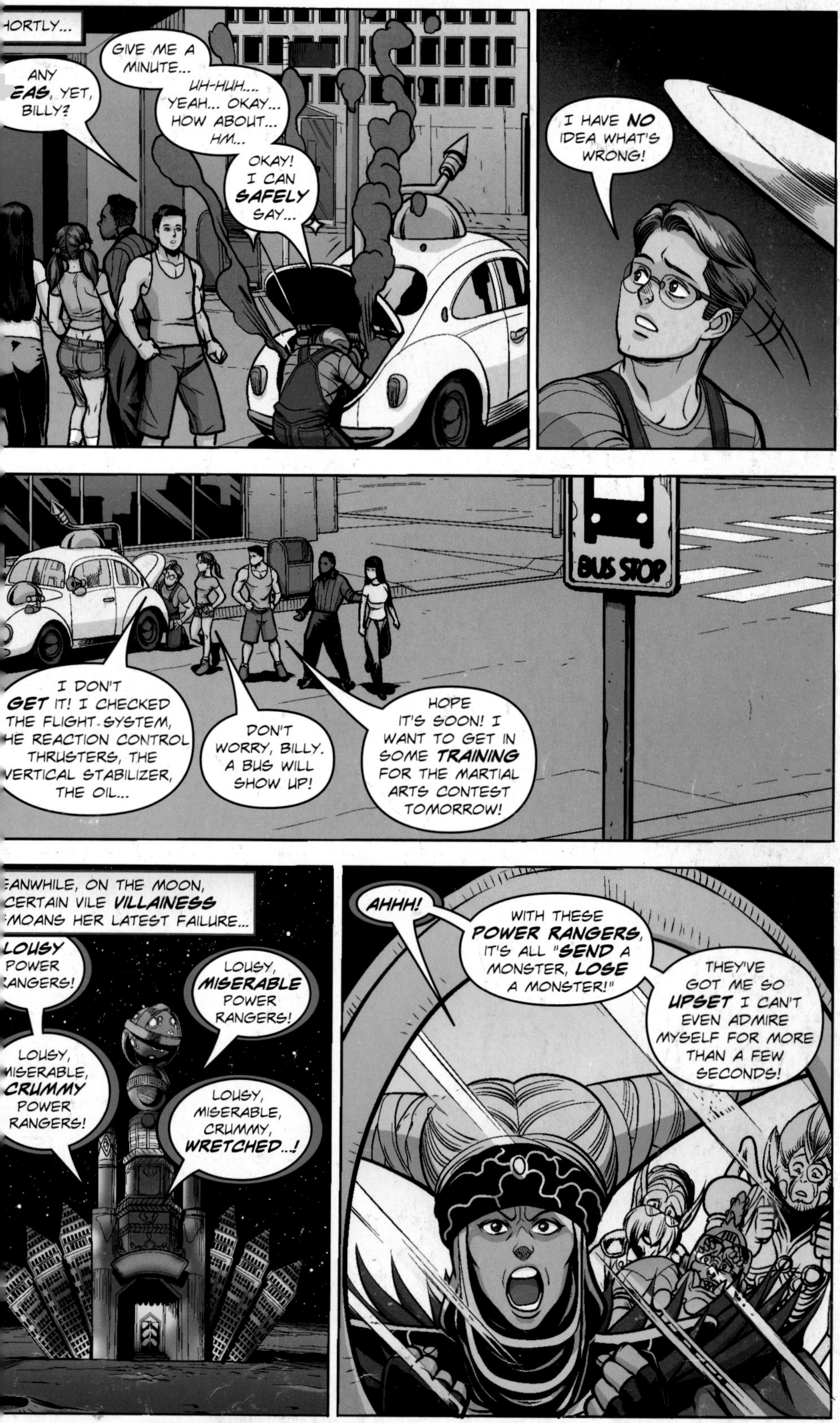

HORTLY...
ANY
EAS, YET, BILLY?
GIVE ME A MINUTE...
UH-HUH.... YEAH... OKAY... HOW ABOUT... HM...
OKAY! I CAN SAFELY SAY...
I HAVE NO IDEA WHAT'S WRONG!
BUS STOP
I DON'T GET IT! I CHECKED THE FLIGHT SYSTEM, HE REACTION CONTROL THRUSTERS, THE VERTICAL STABILIZER, THE OIL...
DON'T WORRY, BILLY. A BUS WILL SHOW UP!
HOPE IT'S SOON! I WANT TO GET IN SOME TRAINING FOR THE MARTIAL ARTS CONTEST TOMORROW!
EANWHILE, ON THE MOON, CERTAIN VILE VILLAINESS EMOANS HER LATEST FAILURE...
LOUSY POWER ANGERS!
LOUSY, MISERABLE POWER RANGERS!
LOUSY, ISERABLE, CRUMMY POWER RANGERS!
LOUSY, MISERABLE, CRUMMY, WRETCHED...!
AHHH!
WITH THESE POWER RANGERS, IT'S ALL "SEND A MONSTER, LOSE A MONSTER!"
THEY'VE GOT ME SO UPSET I CAN'T EVEN ADMIRE MYSELF FOR MORE THAN A FEW SECONDS!

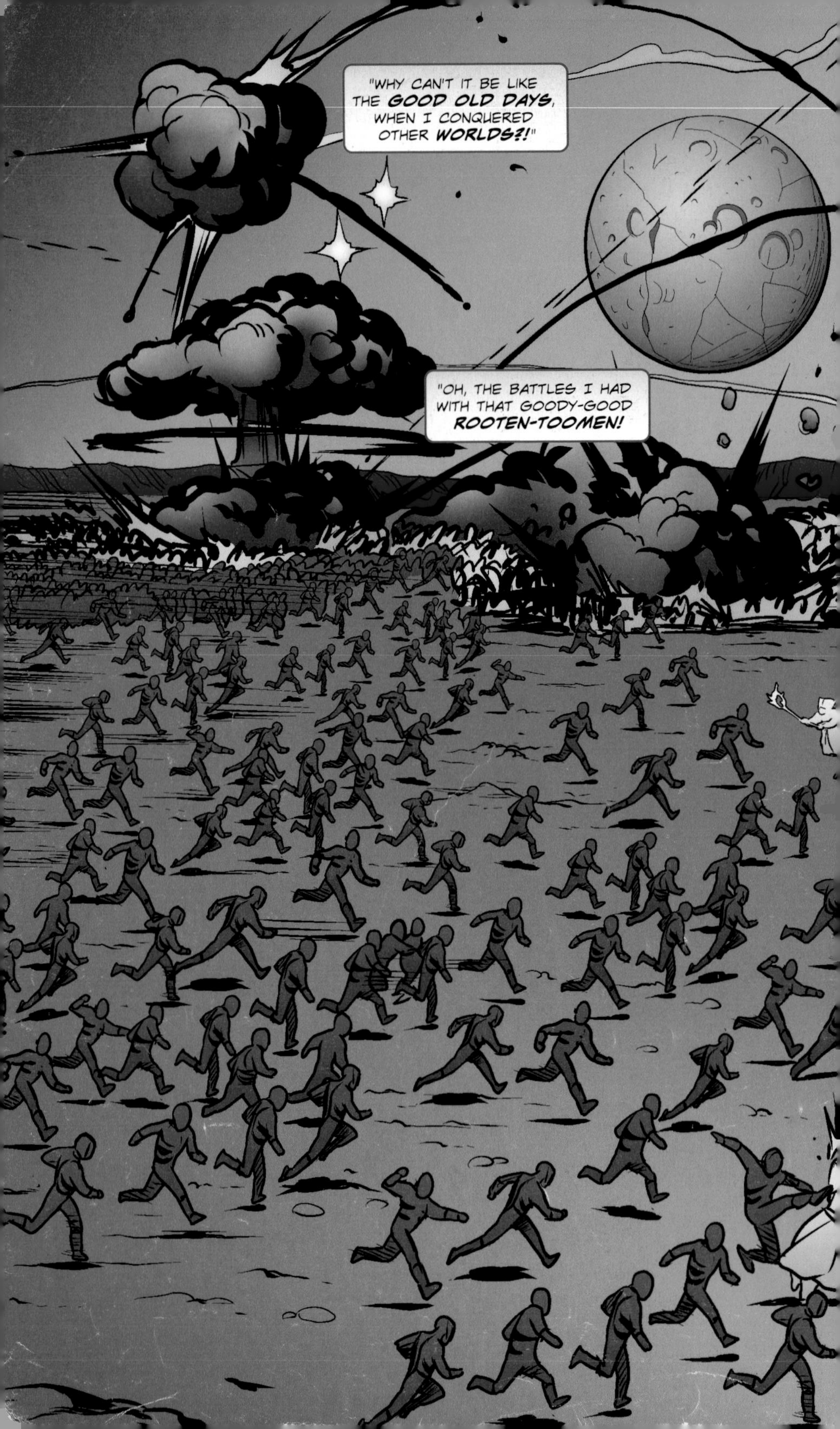
"WHY CAN'T IT BE LIKE THE GOOD OLD DAYS, WHEN I CONQUERED OTHER WORLDS?!"
"OH, THE BATTLES I HAD WITH THAT GOODY-GOOD ROOTEN-TOOMEN!

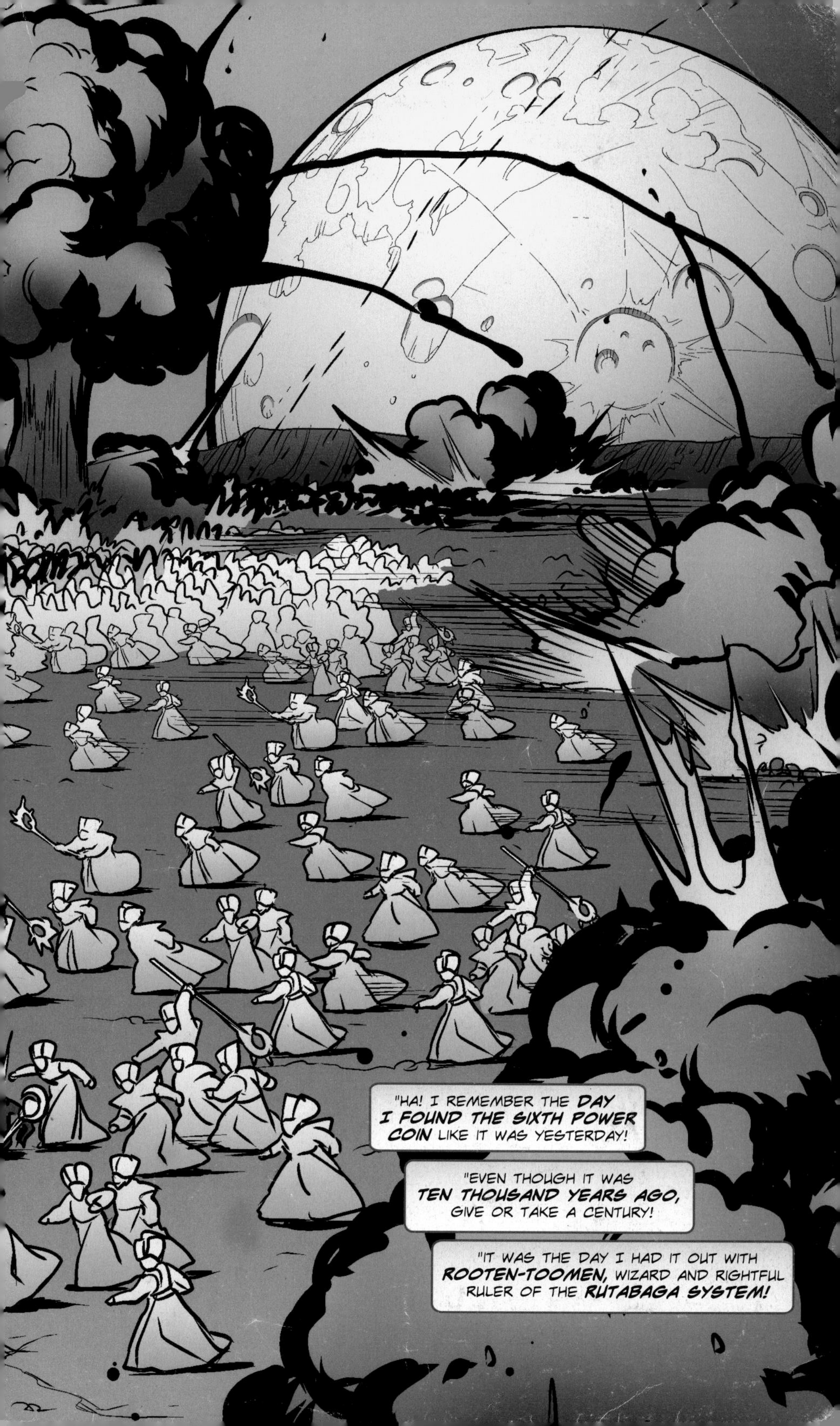
"HA! I REMEMBER THE DAY I FOUND THE SIXTH POWER COIN LIKE IT WAS YESTERDAY!
"EVEN THOUGH IT WAS TEN THOUSAND YEARS AGO, GIVE OR TAKE A CENTURY!
"IT WAS THE DAY I HAD IT OUT WITH ROOTEN-TOOMEN, WIZARD AND RIGHTFUL RULER OF THE RUTABAGA SYSTEM!

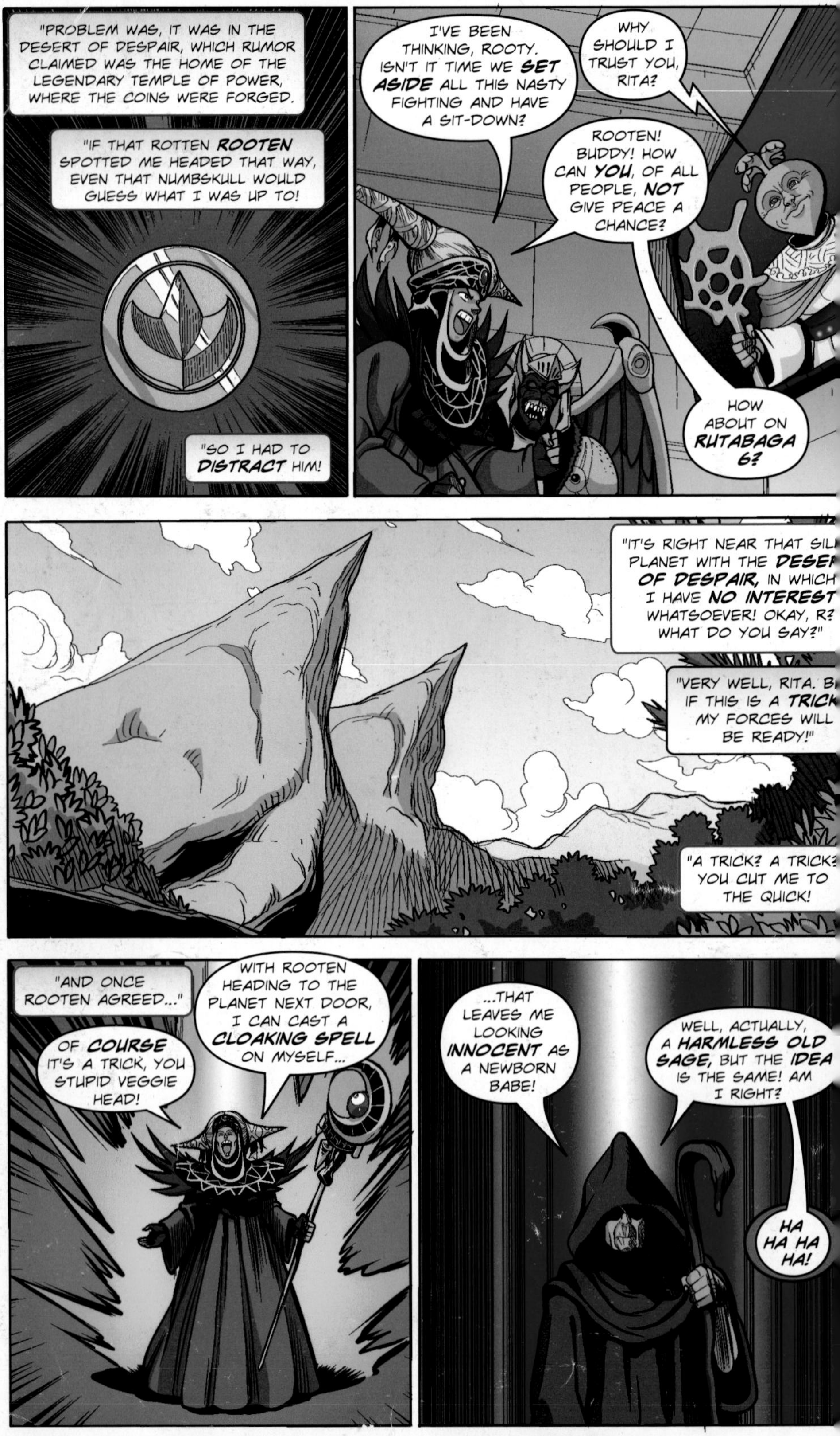

"PROBLEM WAS, IT WAS IN THE DESERT OF DESPAIR, WHICH RUMOR CLAIMED WAS THE HOME OF THE LEGENDARY TEMPLE OF POWER, WHERE THE COINS WERE FORGED.
"IF THAT ROTTEN ROOTEN SPOTTED ME HEADED THAT WAY, EVEN THAT NUMBSKULL WOULD GUESS WHAT I WAS UP TO!
"SO I HAD TO DISTRACT HIM!
I'VE BEEN THINKING, ROOTY. ISN'T IT TIME WE SET ASIDE ALL THIS NASTY FIGHTING AND HAVE A SIT-DOWN?
WHY SHOULD I TRUST YOU, RITA?
ROOTEN! BUDDY! HOW CAN YOU, OF ALL PEOPLE, NOT GIVE PEACE A CHANCE?
HOW ABOUT ON RUTABAGA 6?
"IT'S RIGHT NEAR THAT SIL PLANET WITH THE DESE OF DESPAIR, IN WHICH I HAVE NO INTEREST WHATSOEVER! OKAY, R? WHAT DO YOU SAY?"
"VERY WELL, RITA. B IF THIS IS A TRICK MY FORCES WILL BE READY!"
"A TRICK? A TRICK? YOU CUT ME TO THE QUICK!
"AND ONCE ROOTEN AGREED..."
OF COURSE IT'S A TRICK, YOU STUPID VEGGIE HEAD!
WITH ROOTEN HEADING TO THE PLANET NEXT DOOR, I CAN CAST A CLOAKING SPELL ON MYSELF...
...THAT LEAVES ME LOOKING INNOCENT AS A NEWBORN BABE!
WELL, ACTUALLY, A HARMLESS OLD SAGE, BUT THE IDEA IS THE SAME! AM I RIGHT?
HA HA HA HA!

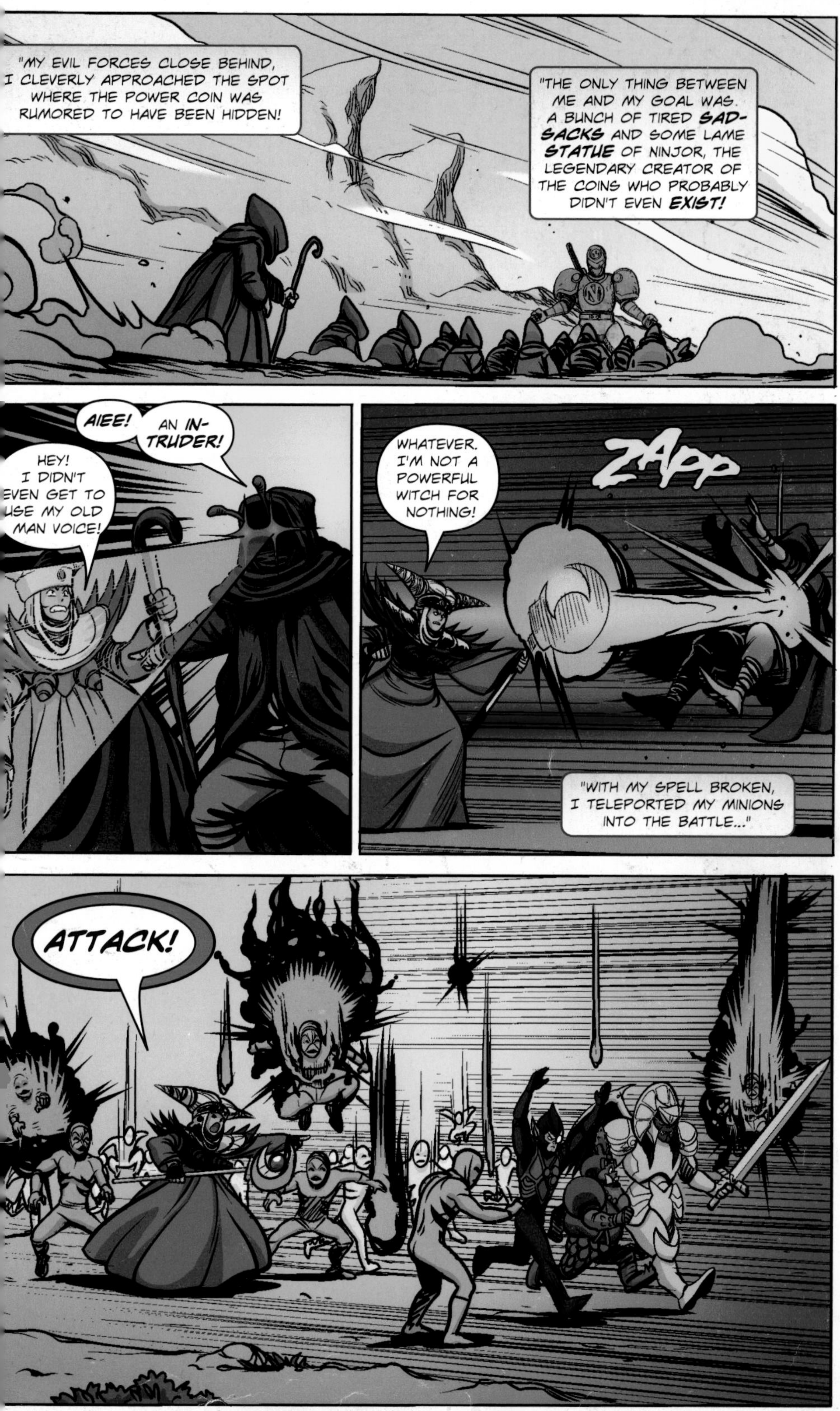
"MY EVIL FORCES CLOSE BEHIND, I CLEVERLY APPROACHED THE SPOT WHERE THE POWER COIN WAS RUMORED TO HAVE BEEN HIDDEN!
"THE ONLY THING BETWEEN ME AND MY GOAL WAS A BUNCH OF TIRED SAD-SACKS AND SOME LAME STATUE OF NINJOR, THE LEGENDARY CREATOR OF THE COINS WHO PROBABLY DIDN'T EVEN EXIST!
AIEE!
AN IN-TRUDER!
HEY! I DIDN'T EVEN GET TO USE MY OLD MAN VOICE!
WHATEVER. I'M NOT A POWERFUL WITCH FOR NOTHING!
ZAPP
"WITH MY SPELL BROKEN, I TELEPORTED MY MINIONS INTO THE BATTLE..."
ATTACK!

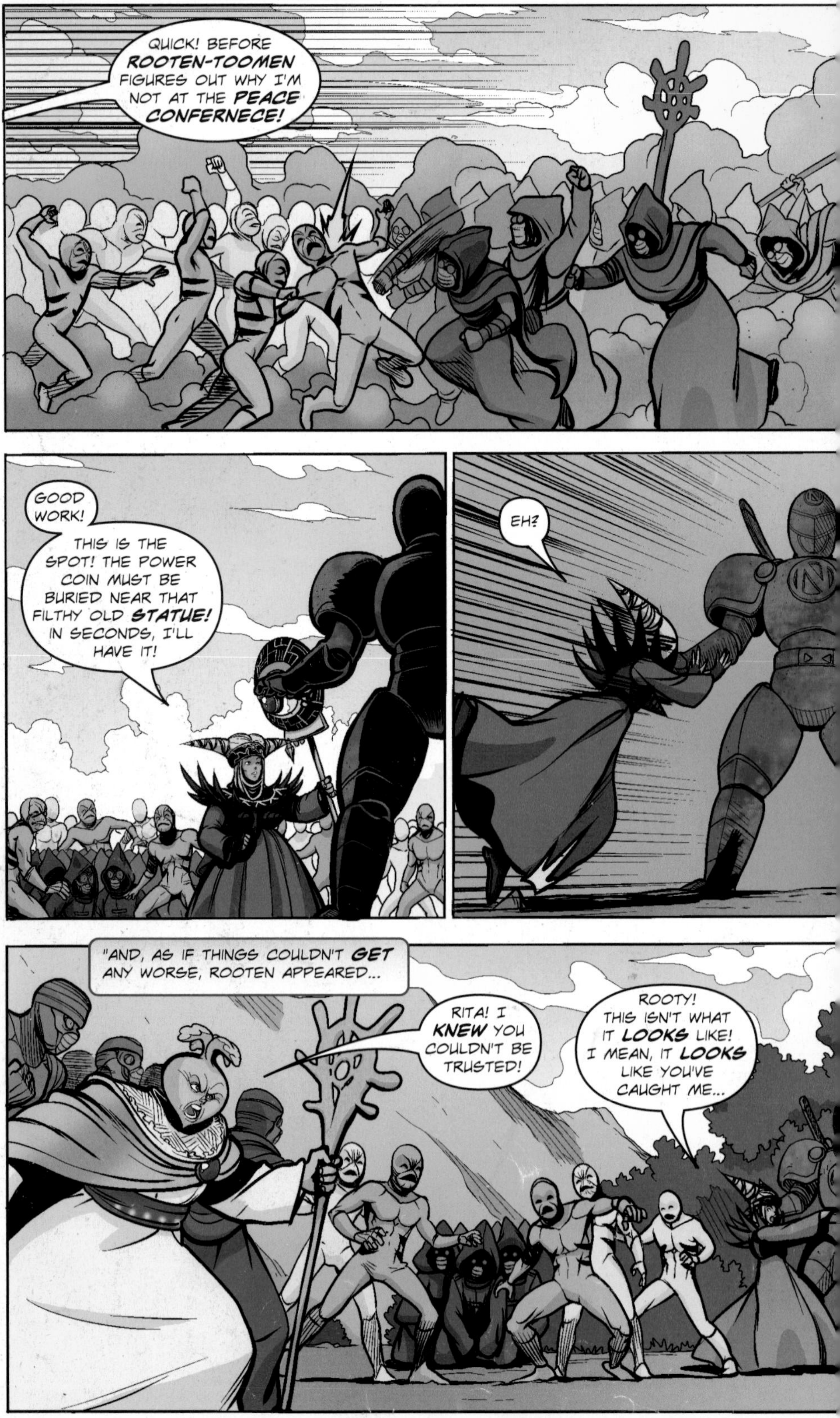
QUICK! BEFORE ROOTEN-TOOMEN FIGURES OUT WHY I'M NOT AT THE PEACE CONFERNECE!
GOOD WORK!
THIS IS THE SPOT! THE POWER COIN MUST BE BURIED NEAR THAT FILTHY OLD STATUE! IN SECONDS, I'LL HAVE IT!
EH?
"AND, AS IF THINGS COULDN'T GET ANY WORSE, ROOTEN APPEARED...
RITA! I KNEW YOU COULDN'T BE TRUSTED!
ROOTY! THIS ISN'T WHAT IT LOOKS LIKE! I MEAN, IT LOOKS LIKE YOU'VE CAUGHT ME...

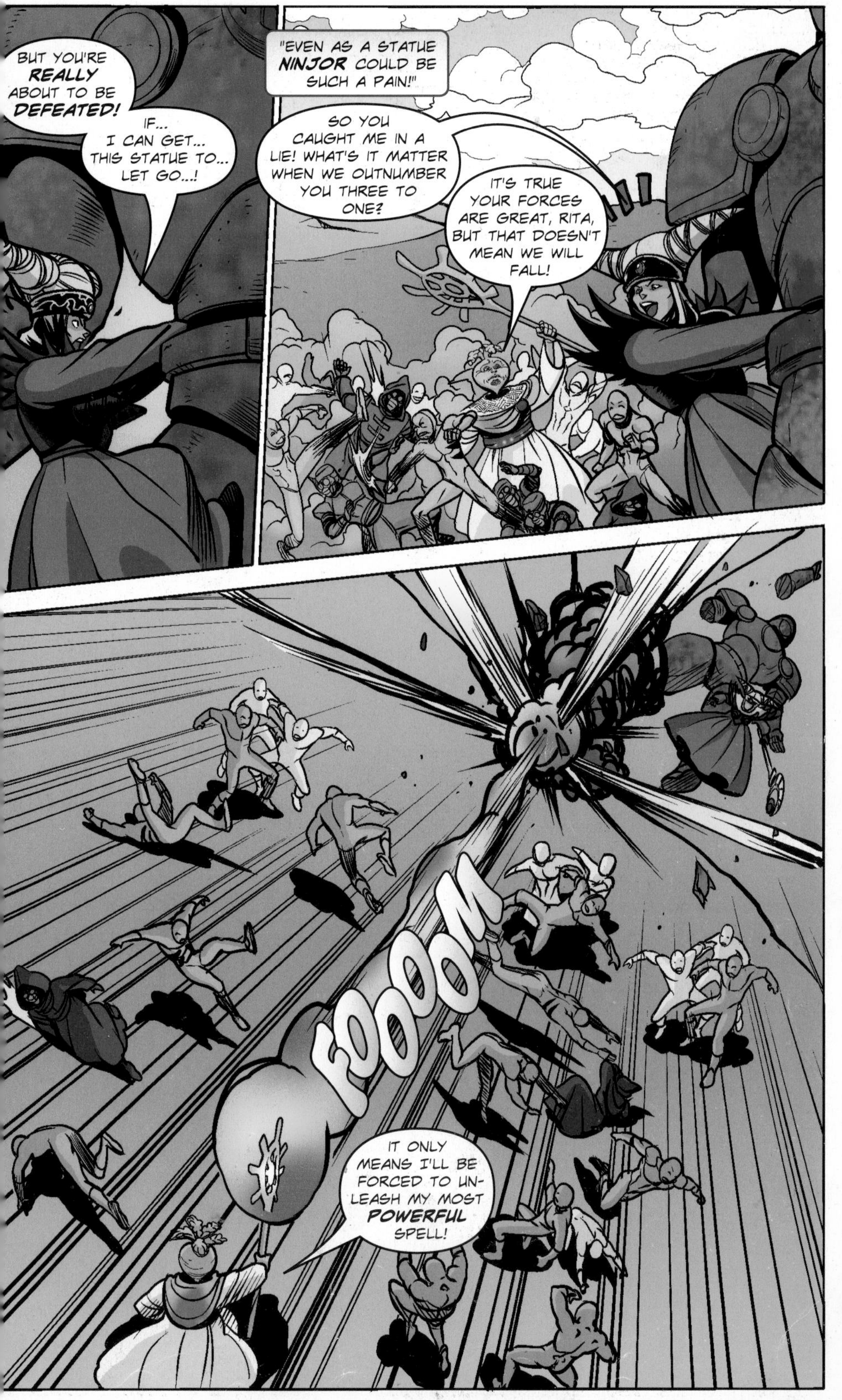
BUT YOU'RE REALLY ABOUT TO BE DEFEATED!
IF... I CAN GET... THIS STATUE TO... LET GO...!
"EVEN AS A STATUE NINJOR COULD BE SUCH A PAIN!"
SO YOU CAUGHT ME IN A LIE! WHAT'S IT MATTER WHEN WE OUTNUMBER YOU THREE TO ONE?
IT'S TRUE YOUR FORCES ARE GREAT, RITA, BUT THAT DOESN'T MEAN WE WILL FALL!
FOOOOM
IT ONLY MEANS I'LL BE FORCED TO UN-LEASH MY MOST POWERFUL SPELL!

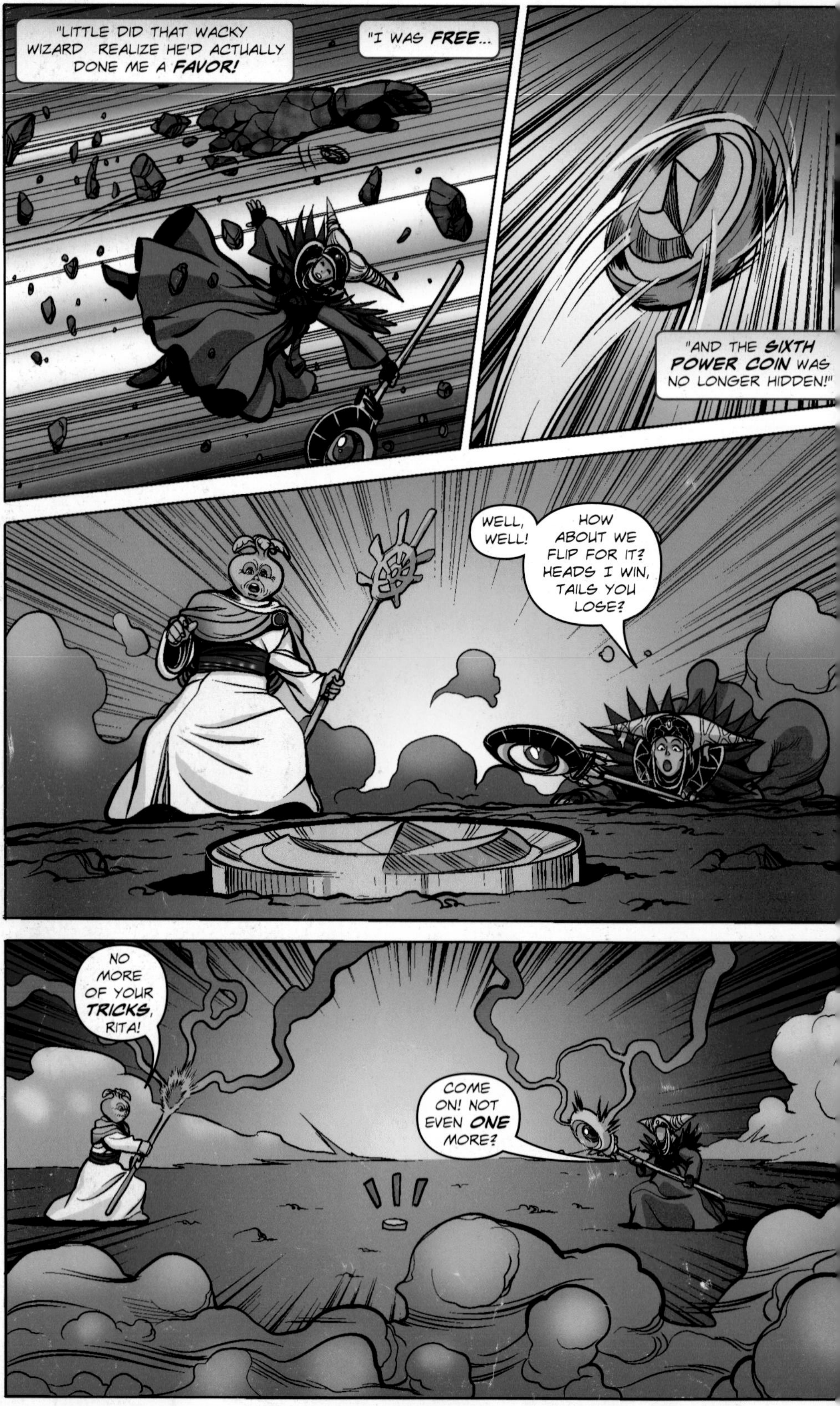
"LITTLE DID THAT WACKY WIZARD REALIZE HE'D ACTUALLY DONE ME A **FAVOR!**
"I WAS **FREE...**
"AND THE **SIXTH POWER COIN** WAS NO LONGER HIDDEN!"
WELL, WELL!
HOW ABOUT WE FLIP FOR IT? HEADS I WIN, TAILS YOU LOSE?
NO MORE OF YOUR **TRICKS**, RITA!
COME ON! NOT EVEN **ONE** MORE?

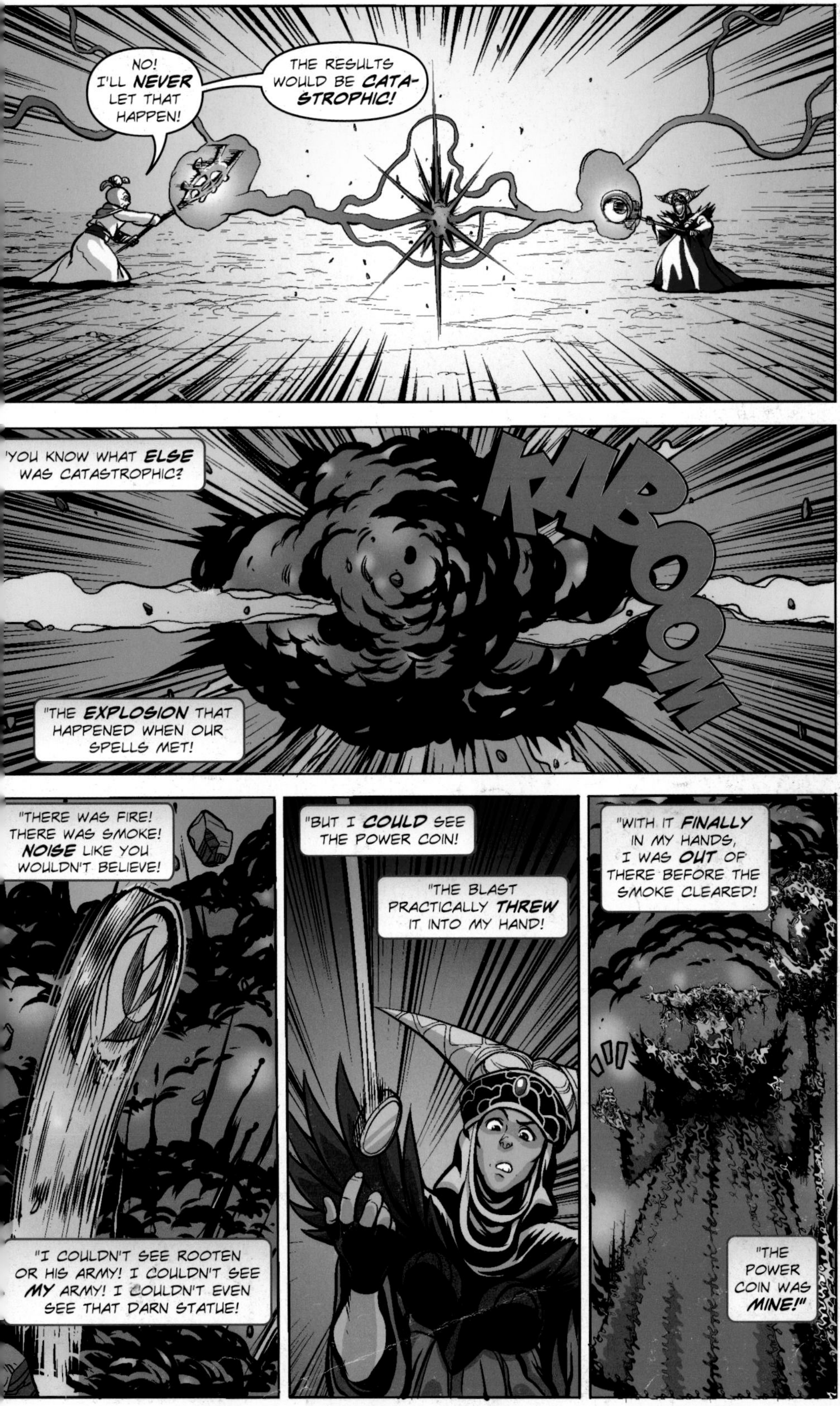
NO! I'LL NEVER LET THAT HAPPEN!
THE RESULTS WOULD BE CATA-STROPHIC!
"YOU KNOW WHAT ELSE WAS CATASTROPHIC?
KABOOM
"THE EXPLOSION THAT HAPPENED WHEN OUR SPELLS MET!
"THERE WAS FIRE! THERE WAS SMOKE! NOISE LIKE YOU WOULDN'T BELIEVE!
"I COULDN'T SEE ROOTEN OR HIS ARMY! I COULDN'T SEE MY ARMY! I COULDN'T EVEN SEE THAT DARN STATUE!
"BUT I COULD SEE THE POWER COIN!
"THE BLAST PRACTICALLY THREW IT INTO MY HAND!
"WITH IT FINALLY IN MY HANDS, I WAS OUT OF THERE BEFORE THE SMOKE CLEARED!
"THE POWER COIN WAS MINE!"

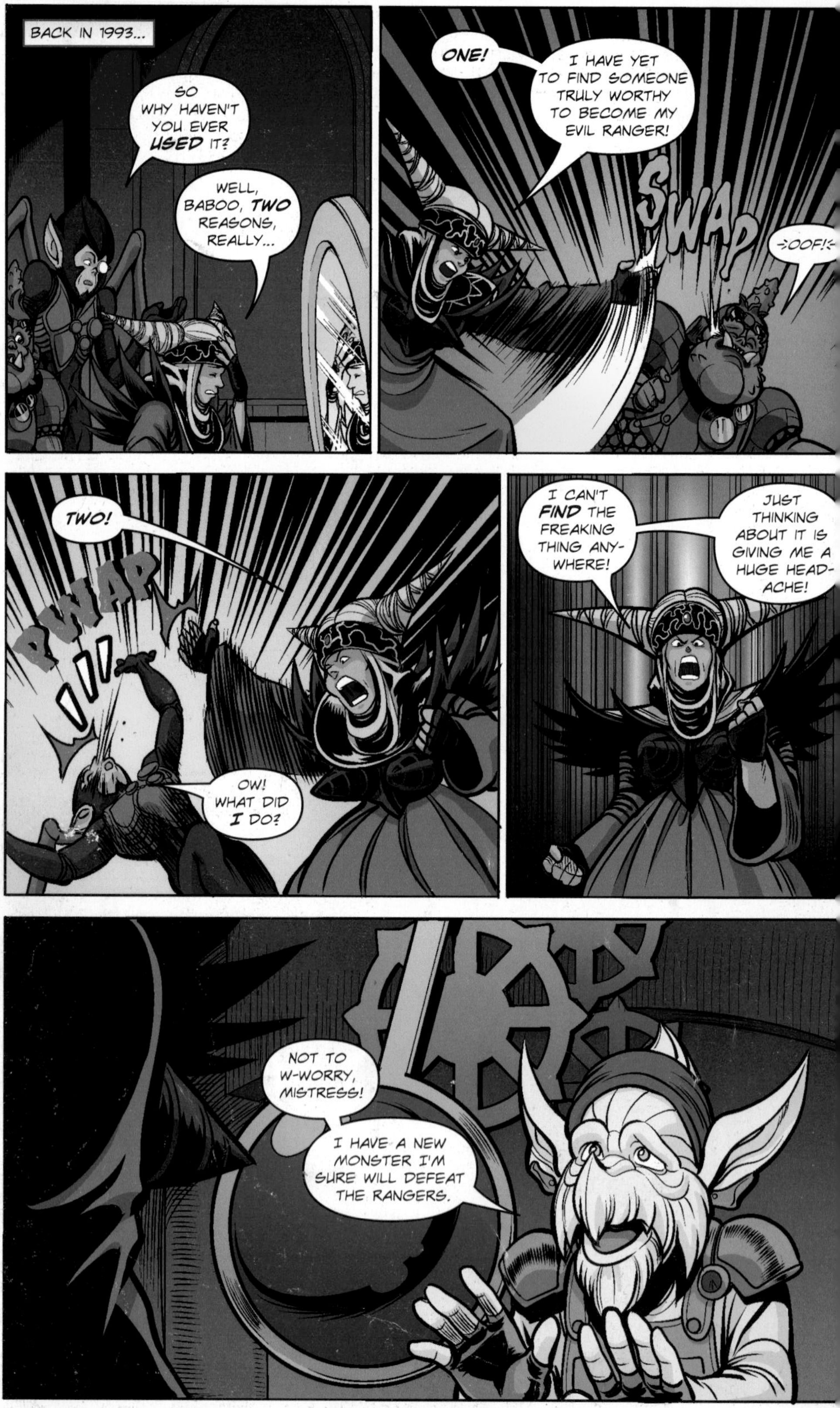
BACK IN 1993...
SO WHY HAVEN'T YOU EVER USED IT?
WELL, BABOO, TWO REASONS, REALLY...
ONE!
I HAVE YET TO FIND SOMEONE TRULY WORTHY TO BECOME MY EVIL RANGER!
SWAP
OOF!
TWO!
PWAP
OW! WHAT DID I DO?
I CAN'T FIND THE FREAKING THING ANY-WHERE!
JUST THINKING ABOUT IT IS GIVING ME A HUGE HEAD-ACHE!
NOT TO W-WORRY, MISTRESS!
I HAVE A NEW MONSTER I'M SURE WILL DEFEAT THE RANGERS.

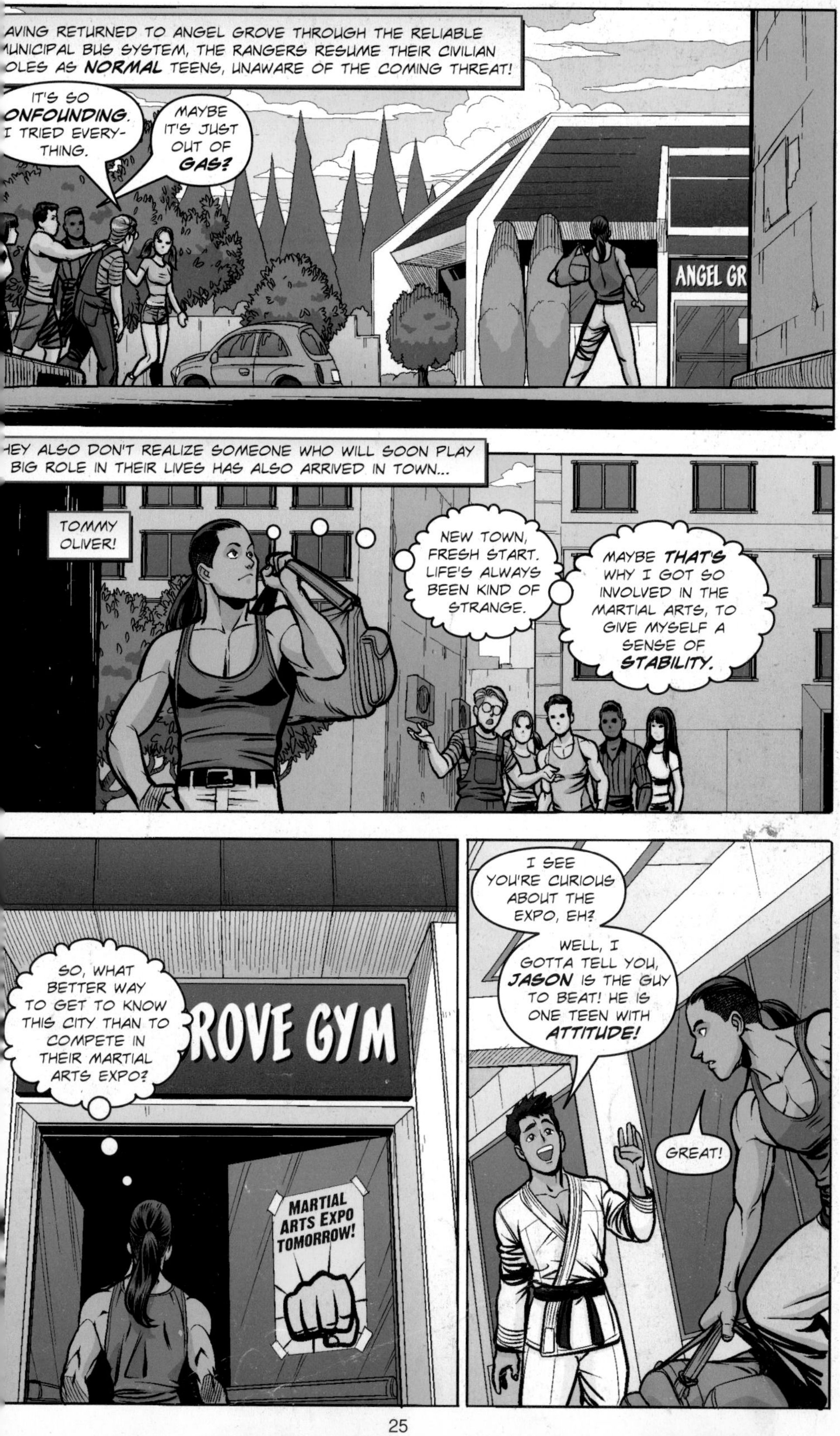
AVING RETURNED TO ANGEL GROVE THROUGH THE RELIABLE
MUNICIPAL BUS SYSTEM, THE RANGERS RESUME THEIR CIVILIAN
OLES AS **NORMAL** TEENS, UNAWARE OF THE COMING THREAT!
IT'S SO **ONFOUNDING**. I TRIED EVERY-THING.
MAYBE IT'S JUST OUT OF **GAS?**
ANGEL GR
HEY ALSO DON'T REALIZE SOMEONE WHO WILL SOON PLAY
BIG ROLE IN THEIR LIVES HAS ALSO ARRIVED IN TOWN...
TOMMY OLIVER!
NEW TOWN, FRESH START. LIFE'S ALWAYS BEEN KIND OF STRANGE.
MAYBE **THAT'S** WHY I GOT SO INVOLVED IN THE MARTIAL ARTS, TO GIVE MYSELF A SENSE OF **STABILITY.**
SO, WHAT BETTER WAY TO GET TO KNOW THIS CITY THAN TO COMPETE IN THEIR MARTIAL ARTS EXPO?
ROVE GYM
MARTIAL ARTS EXPO TOMORROW!
I SEE YOU'RE CURIOUS ABOUT THE EXPO, EH?
WELL, I GOTTA TELL YOU, **JASON** IS THE GUY TO BEAT! HE IS ONE TEEN WITH **ATTITUDE!**
GREAT!

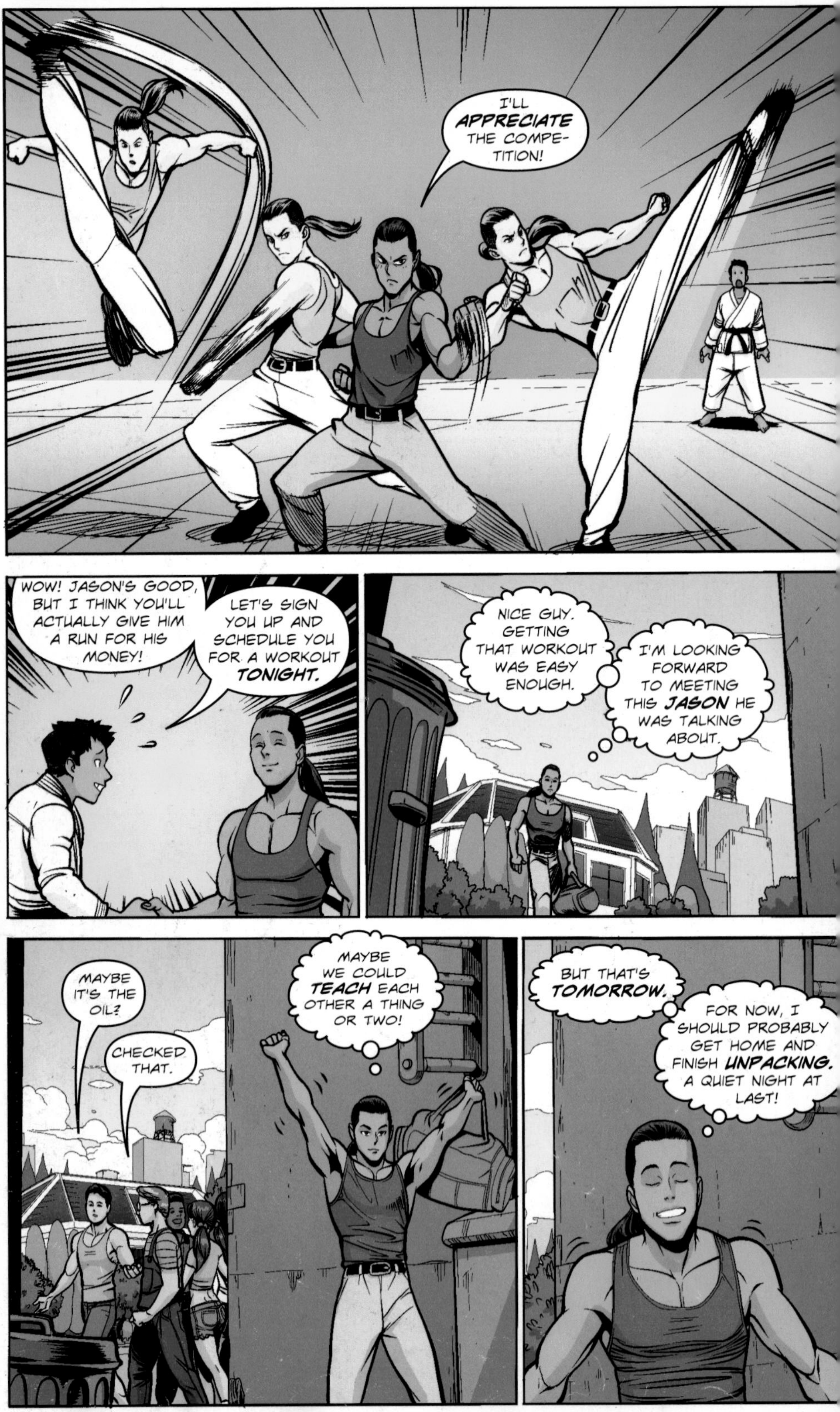
I'LL APPRECIATE THE COMPETITION!
WOW! JASON'S GOOD, BUT I THINK YOU'LL ACTUALLY GIVE HIM A RUN FOR HIS MONEY!
LET'S SIGN YOU UP AND SCHEDULE YOU FOR A WORKOUT TONIGHT.
NICE GUY. GETTING THAT WORKOUT WAS EASY ENOUGH.
I'M LOOKING FORWARD TO MEETING THIS JASON HE WAS TALKING ABOUT.
MAYBE IT'S THE OIL?
CHECKED THAT.
MAYBE WE COULD TEACH EACH OTHER A THING OR TWO!
BUT THAT'S TOMORROW.
FOR NOW, I SHOULD PROBABLY GET HOME AND FINISH UNPACKING. A QUIET NIGHT AT LAST!

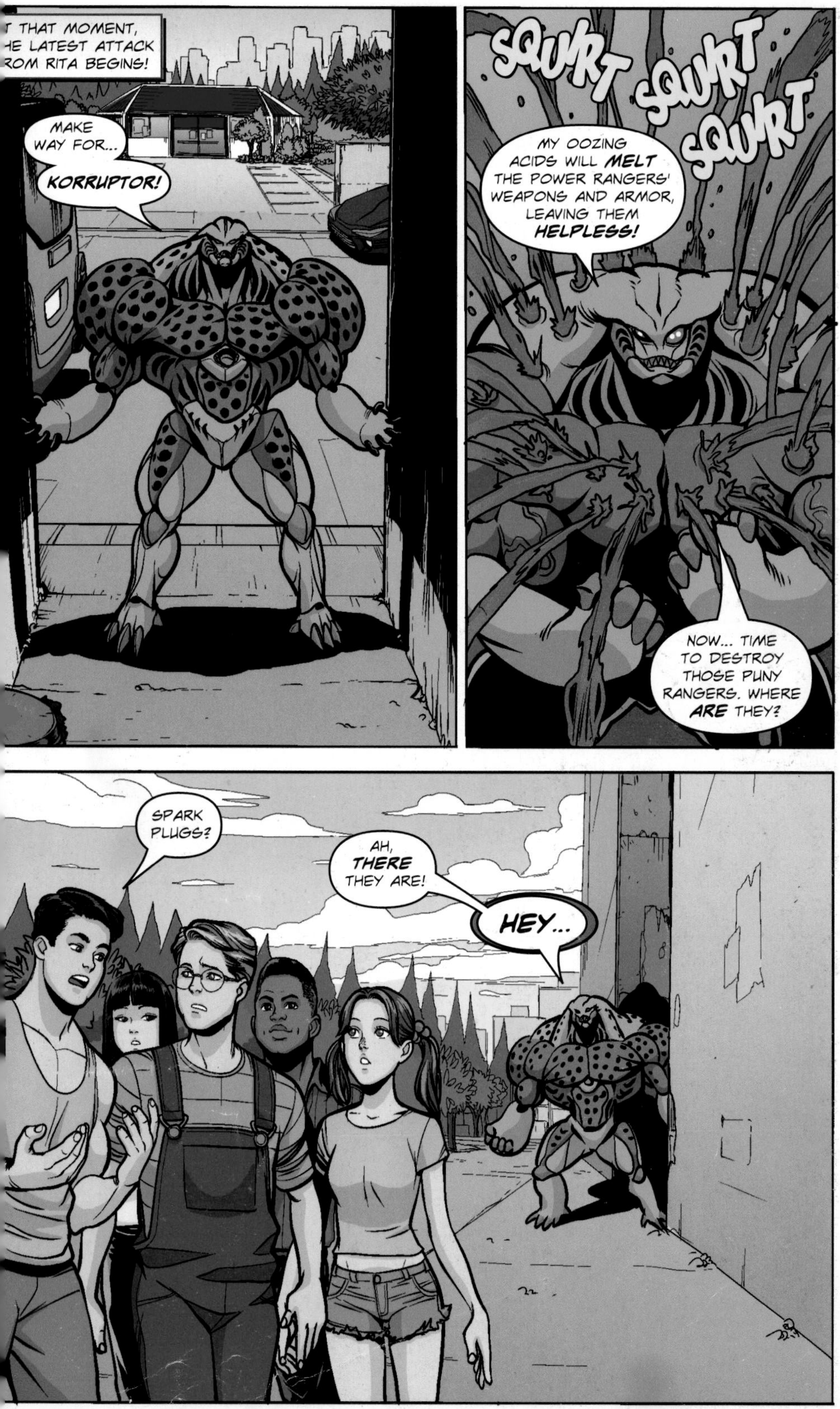
T THAT MOMENT, HE LATEST ATTACK ROM RITA BEGINS!
MAKE WAY FOR...
KORRUPTOR!
SQUIRT SQUIRT SQUIRT
MY OOZING ACIDS WILL MELT THE POWER RANGERS' WEAPONS AND ARMOR, LEAVING THEM HELPLESS!
NOW... TIME TO DESTROY THOSE PUNY RANGERS. WHERE ARE THEY?
SPARK PLUGS?
AH, THERE THEY ARE!
HEY...

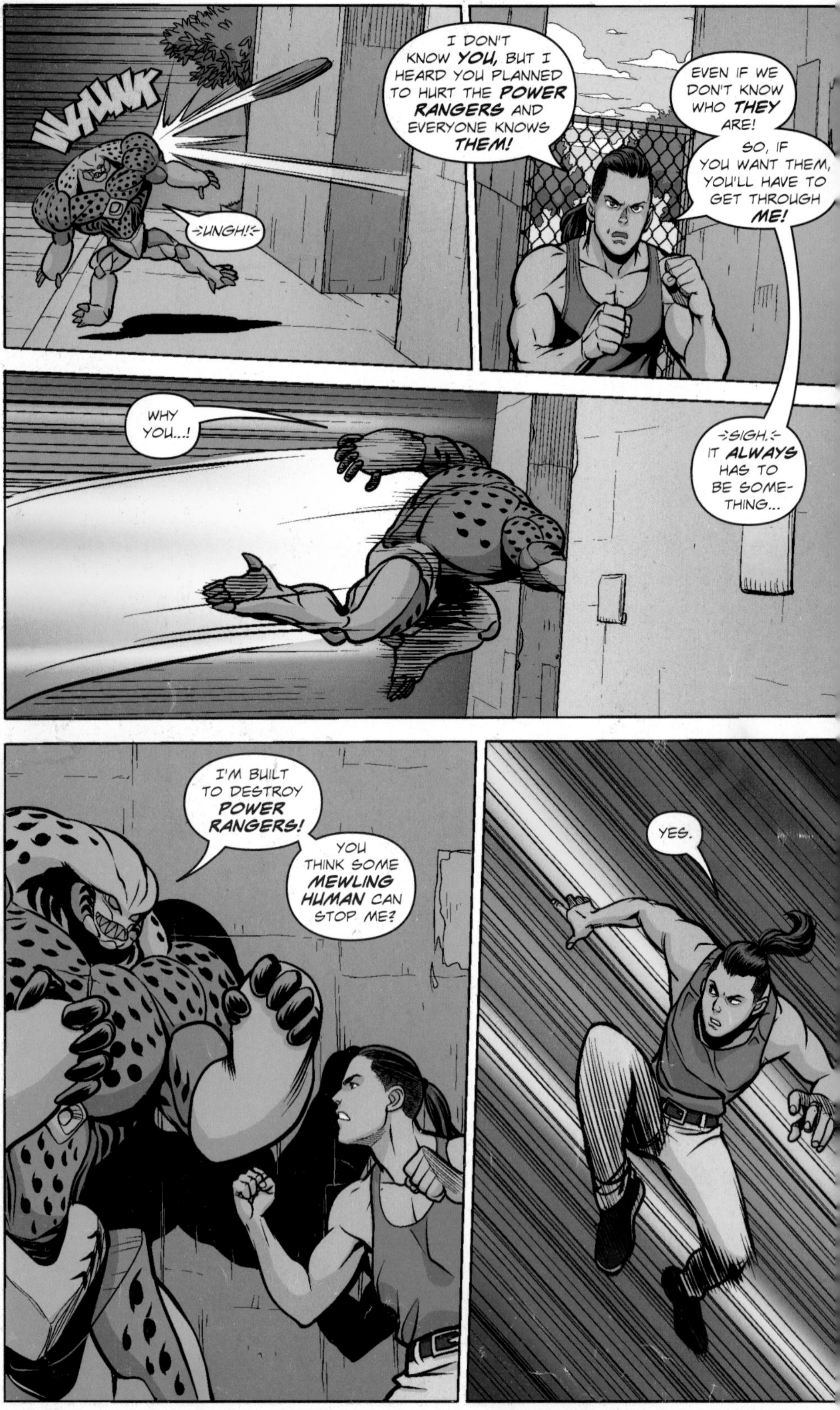
WHUNK
-UNGH!-
I DON'T KNOW YOU, BUT I HEARD YOU PLANNED TO HURT THE POWER RANGERS AND EVERYONE KNOWS THEM!
EVEN IF WE DON'T KNOW WHO THEY ARE!
SO, IF YOU WANT THEM, YOU'LL HAVE TO GET THROUGH ME!
WHY YOU...!
-SIGH.- IT ALWAYS HAS TO BE SOME-THING...
I'M BUILT TO DESTROY POWER RANGERS!
YOU THINK SOME MEWLING HUMAN CAN STOP ME?
YES.

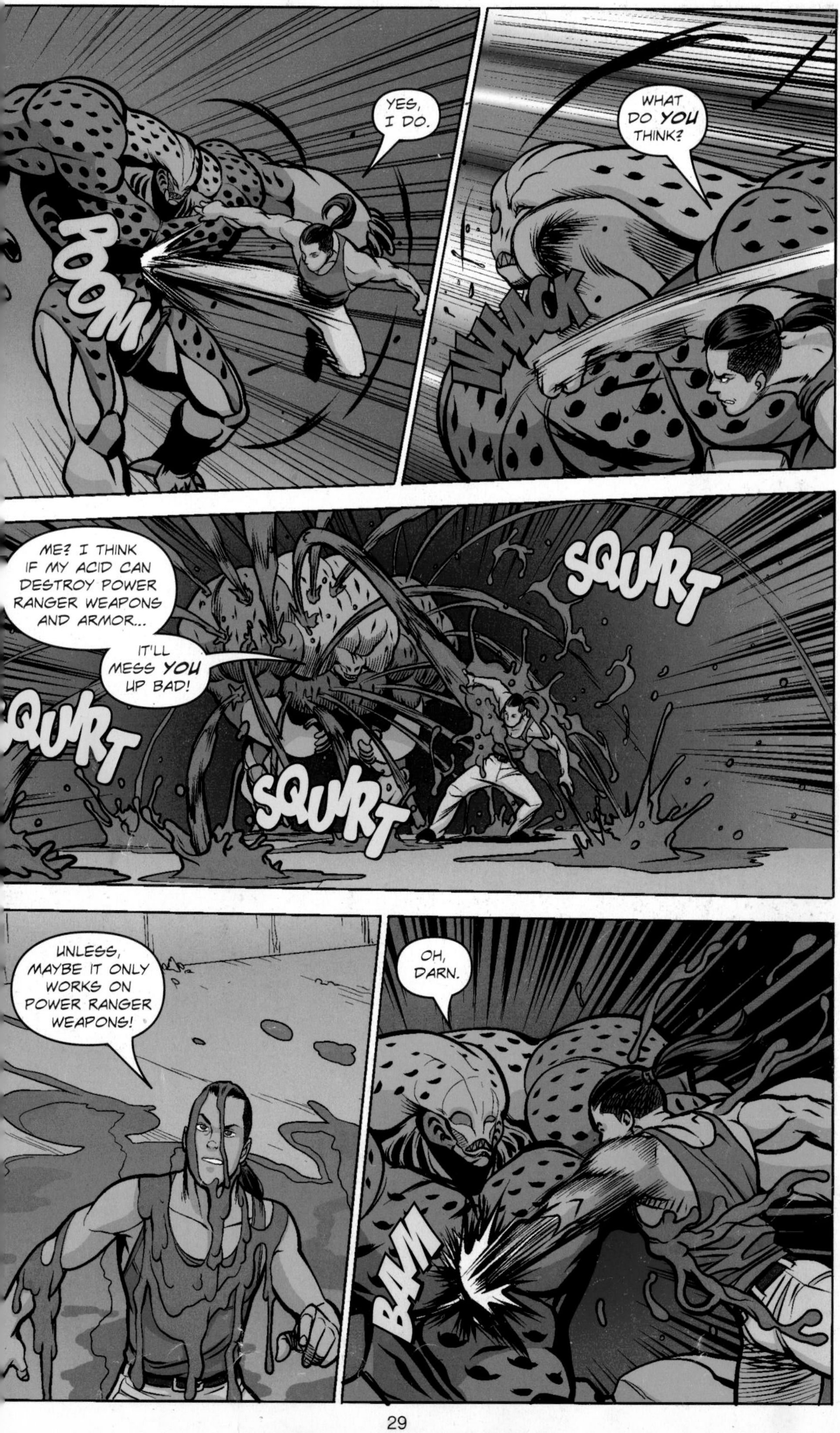
YES, I DO.
BOOM
WHAT DO YOU THINK?
WHACK
ME? I THINK IF MY ACID CAN DESTROY POWER RANGER WEAPONS AND ARMOR...
IT'LL MESS YOU UP BAD!
SQUIRT
SQUIRT
SQUIRT
UNLESS, MAYBE IT ONLY WORKS ON POWER RANGER WEAPONS!
OH, DARN.
BAM

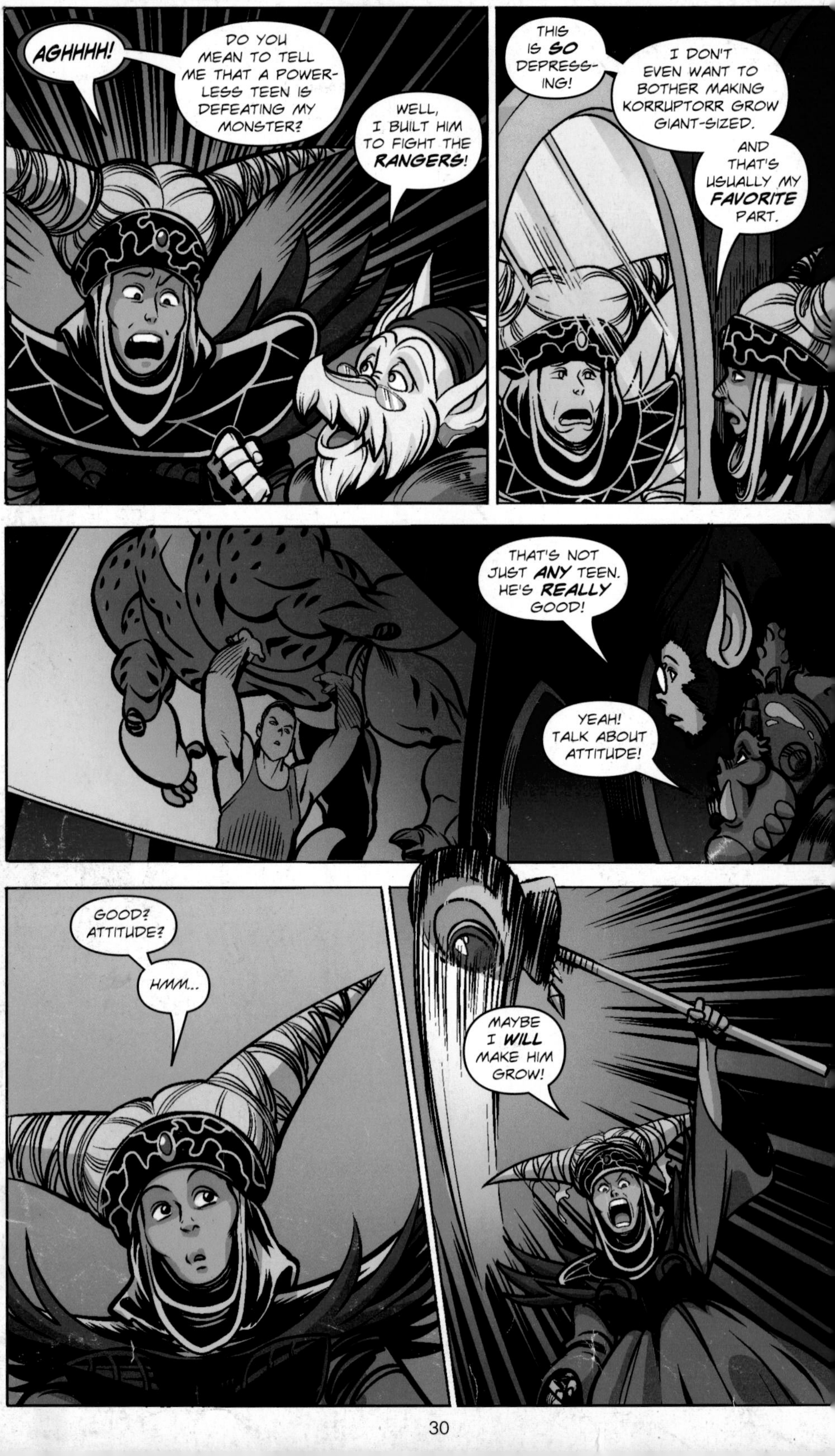
AGHHHH!
DO YOU MEAN TO TELL ME THAT A POWER-LESS TEEN IS DEFEATING MY MONSTER?
WELL, I BUILT HIM TO FIGHT THE RANGERS!
THIS IS SO DEPRESS-ING!
I DON'T EVEN WANT TO BOTHER MAKING KORRUPTORR GROW GIANT-SIZED.
AND THAT'S USUALLY MY FAVORITE PART.
THAT'S NOT JUST ANY TEEN. HE'S REALLY GOOD!
YEAH! TALK ABOUT ATTITUDE!
GOOD? ATTITUDE?
HMM...
MAYBE I WILL MAKE HIM GROW!

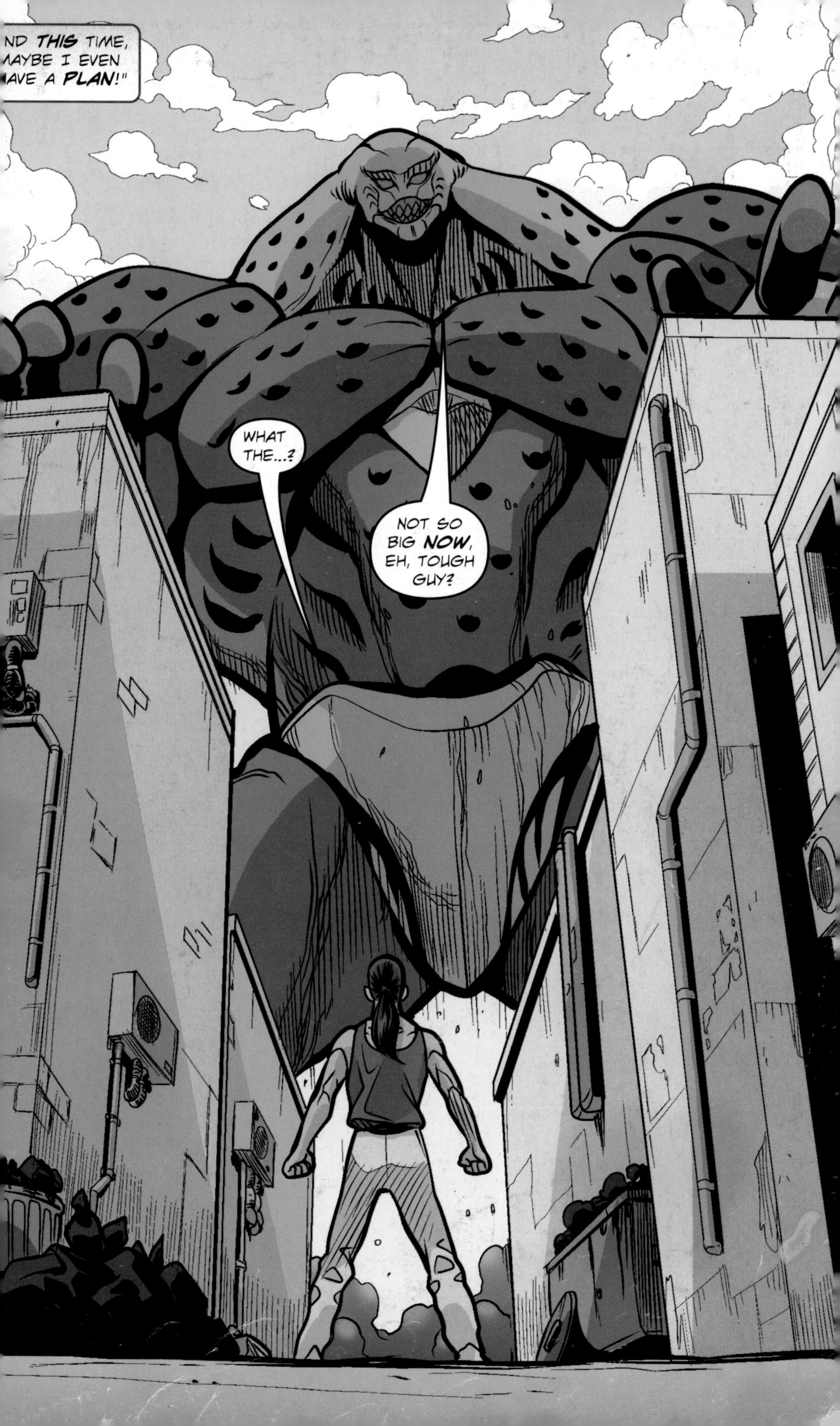
ND THIS TIME, AAYBE I EVEN AVE A PLAN!"
WHAT THE...?
NOT SO BIG NOW, EH, TOUGH GUY?

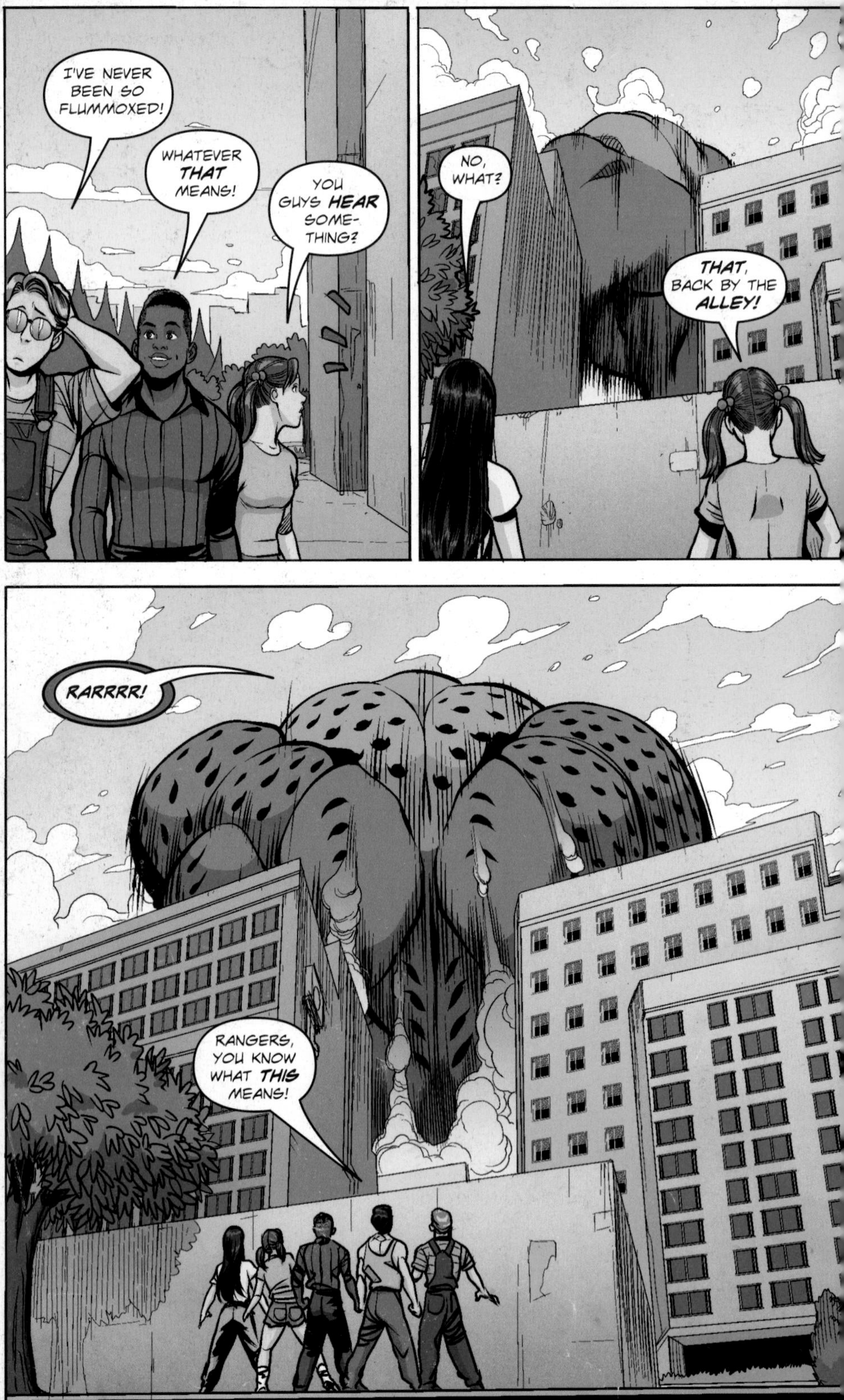
I'VE NEVER BEEN SO FLUMMOXED!
WHATEVER THAT MEANS!
YOU GUYS HEAR SOME-THING?
NO, WHAT?
THAT, BACK BY THE ALLEY!
RARRRR!
RANGERS, YOU KNOW WHAT THIS MEANS!

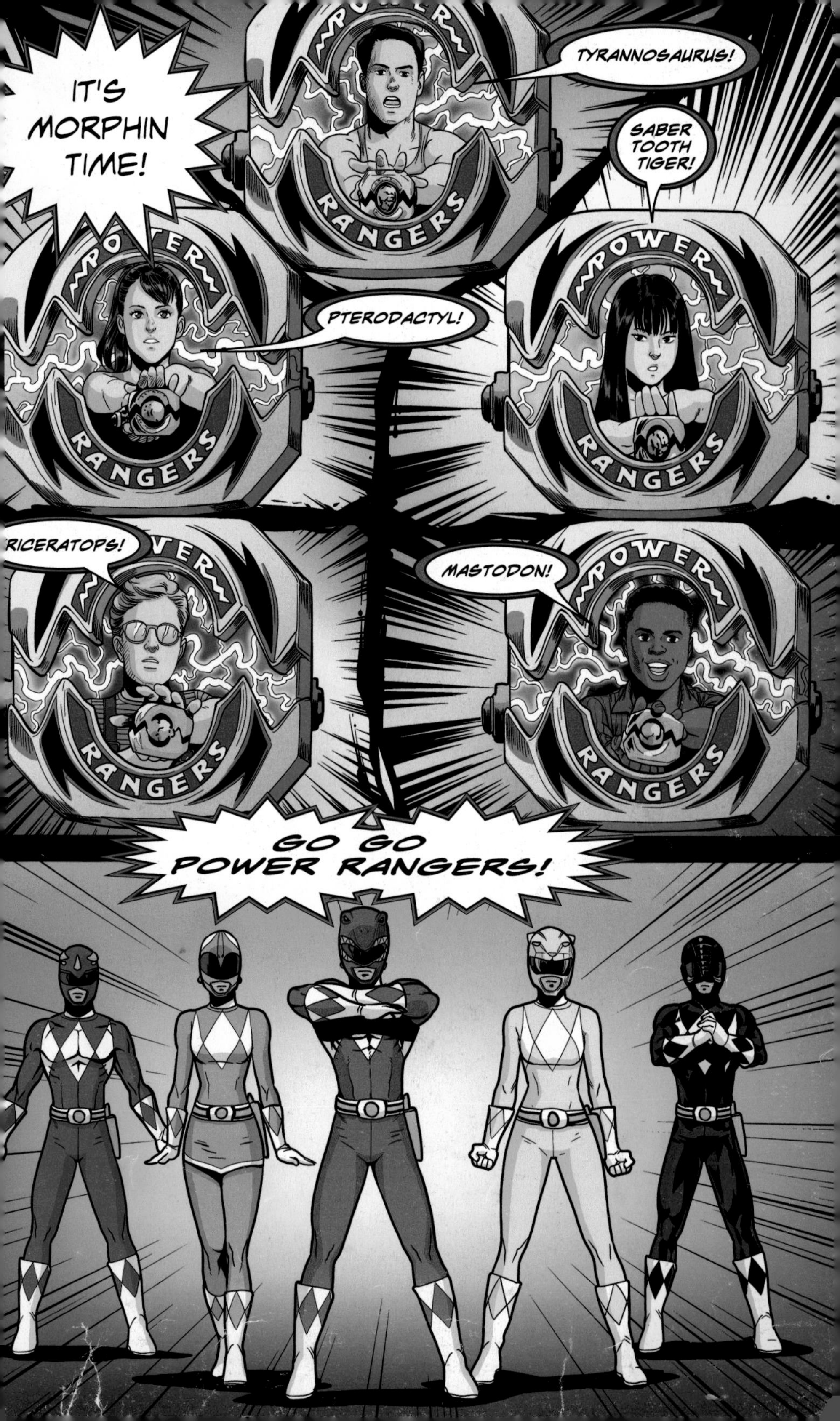
IT'S MORPHIN TIME!
TYRANNOSAURUS!
SABER TOOTH TIGER!
PTERODACTYL!
RICERATOPS!
MASTODON!
GO GO POWER RANGERS!

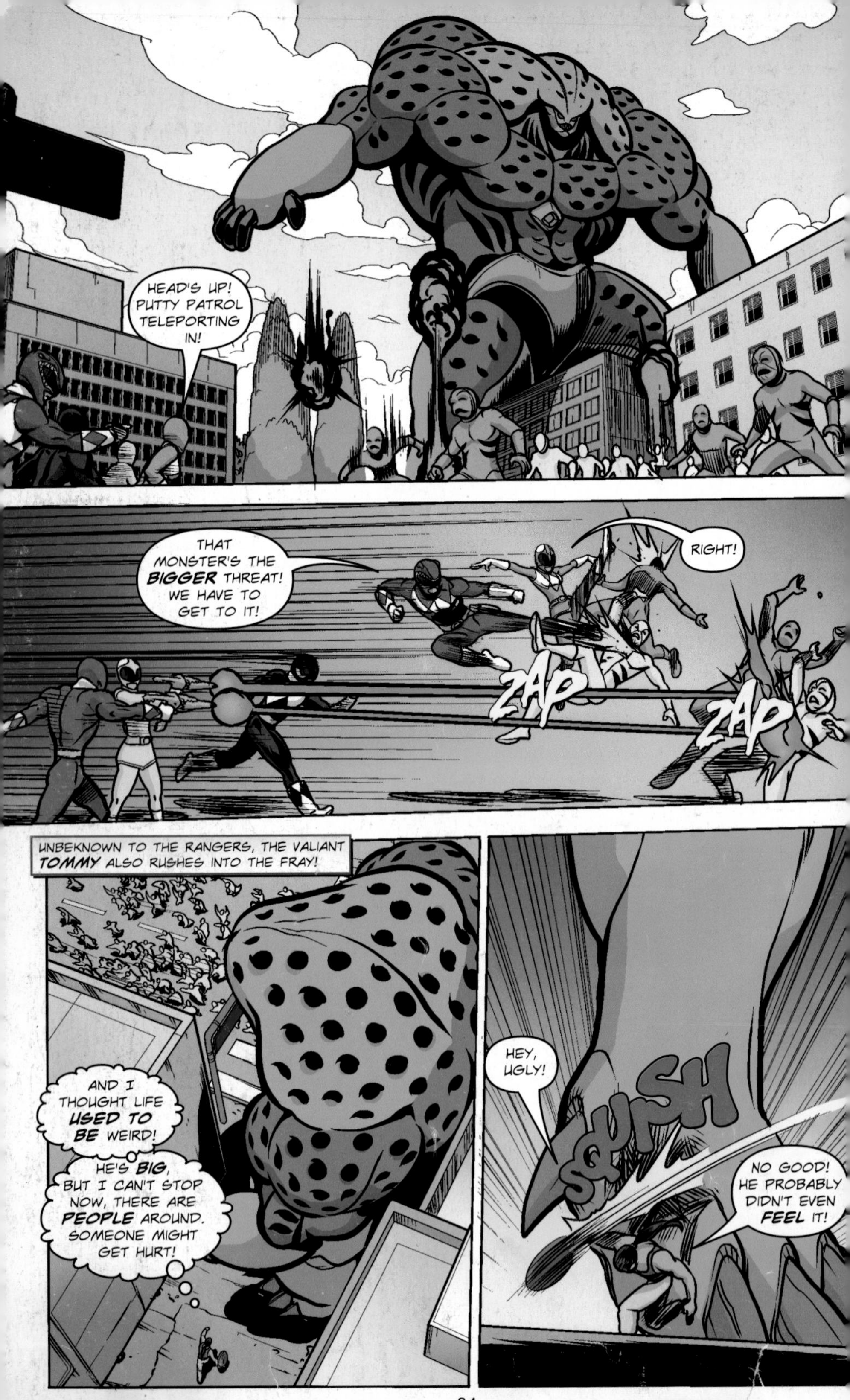
HEAD'S UP! PUTTY PATROL TELEPORTING IN!
THAT MONSTER'S THE BIGGER THREAT! WE HAVE TO GET TO IT!
RIGHT!
ZAP
ZAP
UNBEKNOWN TO THE RANGERS, THE VALIANT TOMMY ALSO RUSHES INTO THE FRAY!
AND I THOUGHT LIFE USED TO BE WEIRD!
HE'S BIG, BUT I CAN'T STOP NOW, THERE ARE PEOPLE AROUND. SOMEONE MIGHT GET HURT!
HEY, UGLY!
SQUISH
NO GOOD! HE PROBABLY DIDN'T EVEN FEEL IT!

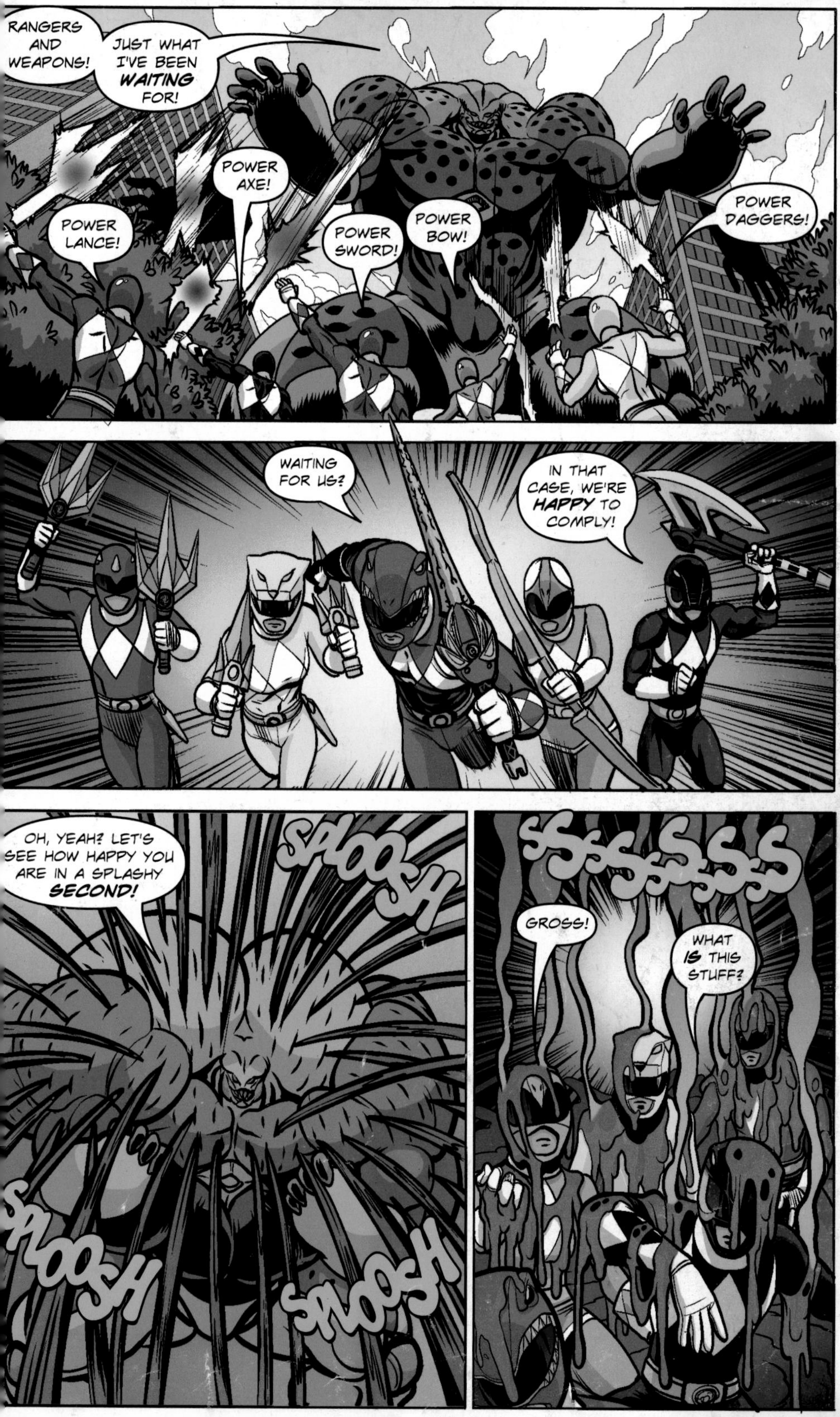
RANGERS AND WEAPONS!
JUST WHAT I'VE BEEN WAITING FOR!
POWER LANCE!
POWER AXE!
POWER SWORD!
POWER BOW!
POWER DAGGERS!
WAITING FOR US?
IN THAT CASE, WE'RE HAPPY TO COMPLY!
OH, YEAH? LET'S SEE HOW HAPPY YOU ARE IN A SPLASHY SECOND!
SPLOOSH
SPLOOSH
SPLOOSH
SSSSSSSSS
GROSS!
WHAT IS THIS STUFF?

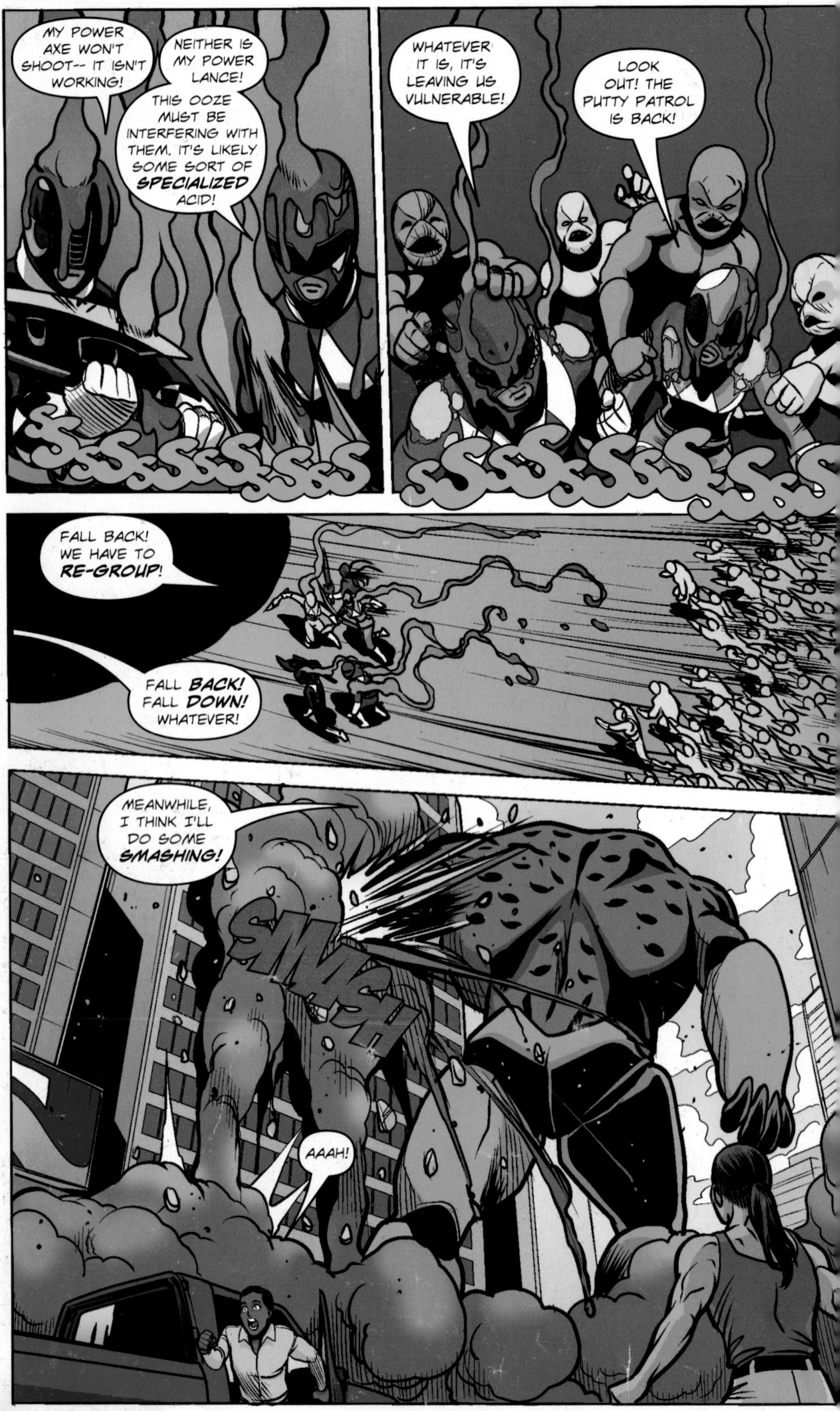

MY POWER AXE WON'T SHOOT-- IT ISN'T WORKING!
NEITHER IS MY POWER LANCE!
THIS OOZE MUST BE INTERFERING WITH THEM. IT'S LIKELY SOME SORT OF SPECIALIZED ACID!
SSSSSSSSSS
WHATEVER IT IS, IT'S LEAVING US VULNERABLE!
LOOK OUT! THE PUTTY PATROL IS BACK!
SSSSSSSSSSSS
FALL BACK! WE HAVE TO RE-GROUP!
FALL BACK! FALL DOWN! WHATEVER!
MEANWHILE, I THINK I'LL DO SOME SMASHING!
SMASH
AAAH!

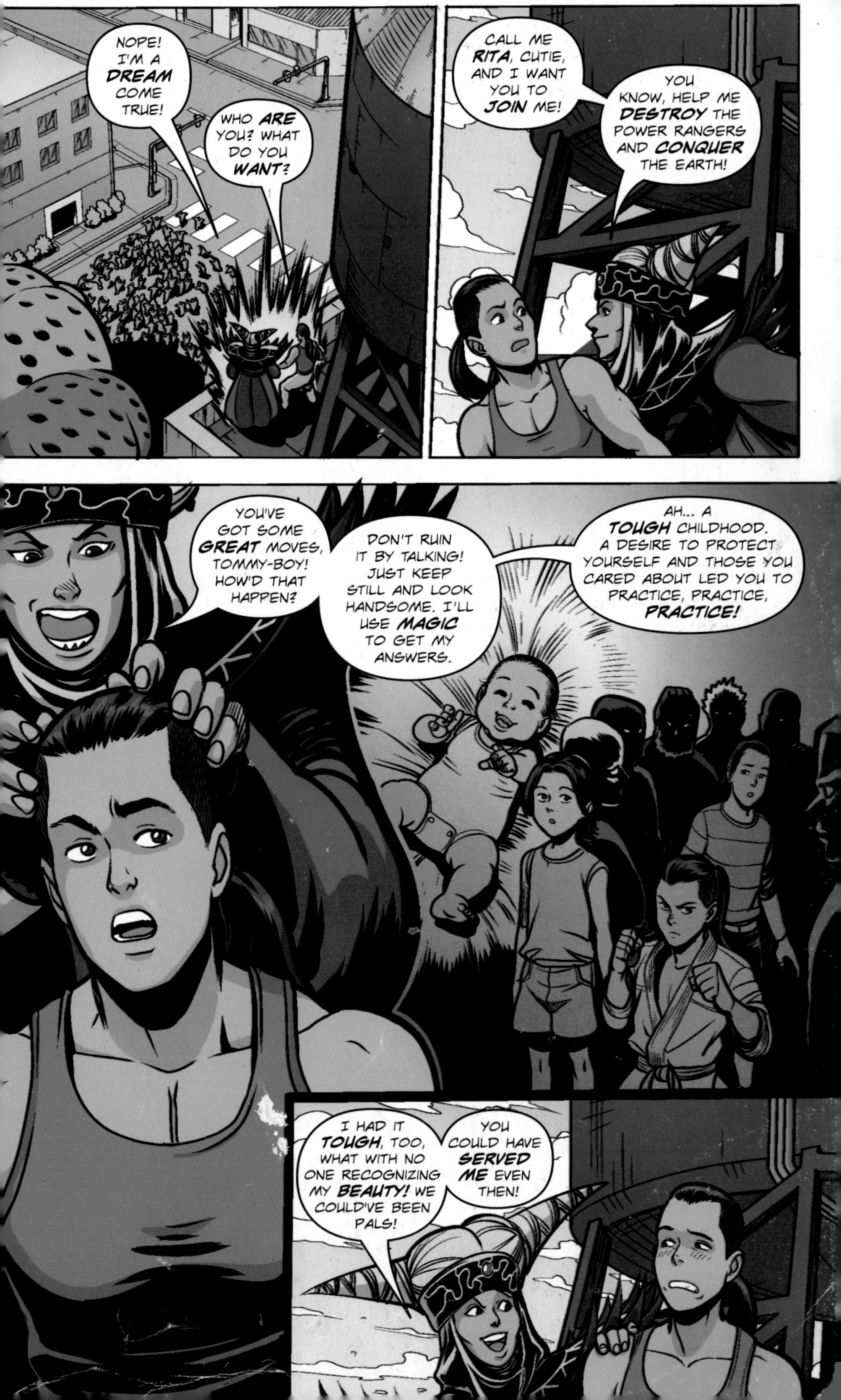
NOPE! I'M A DREAM COME TRUE!
WHO ARE YOU? WHAT DO YOU WANT?
CALL ME RITA, CUTIE, AND I WANT YOU TO JOIN ME!
YOU KNOW, HELP ME DESTROY THE POWER RANGERS AND CONQUER THE EARTH!
YOU'VE GOT SOME GREAT MOVES, TOMMY-BOY! HOW'D THAT HAPPEN?
DON'T RUIN IT BY TALKING! JUST KEEP STILL AND LOOK HANDSOME. I'LL USE MAGIC TO GET MY ANSWERS.
AH... A TOUGH CHILDHOOD. A DESIRE TO PROTECT YOURSELF AND THOSE YOU CARED ABOUT LED YOU TO PRACTICE, PRACTICE, PRACTICE!
I HAD IT TOUGH, TOO, WHAT WITH NO ONE RECOGNIZING MY BEAUTY! WE COULD'VE BEEN PALS!
YOU COULD HAVE SERVED ME EVEN THEN!

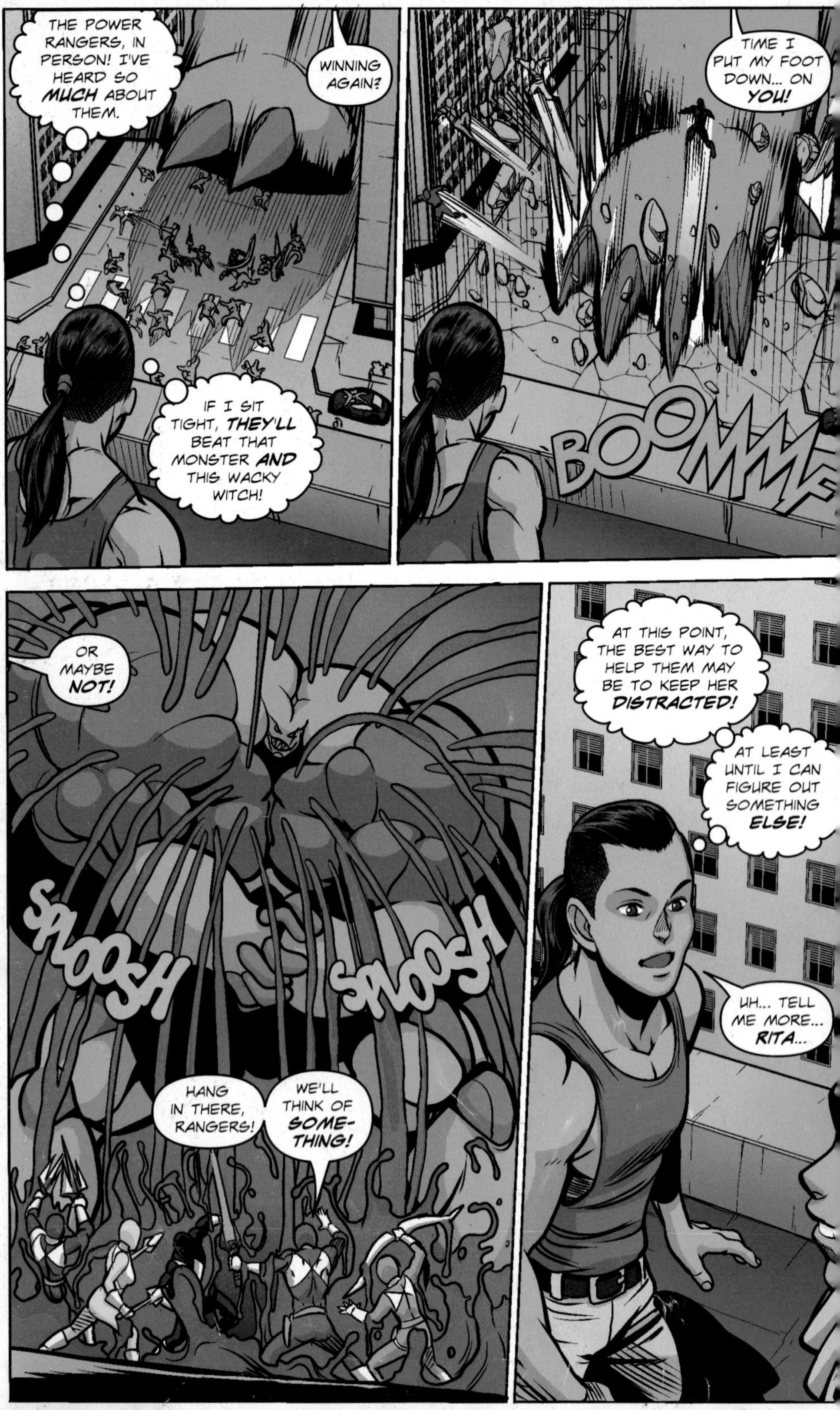
THE POWER RANGERS, IN PERSON! I'VE HEARD SO MUCH ABOUT THEM.
WINNING AGAIN?
IF I SIT TIGHT, THEY'LL BEAT THAT MONSTER AND THIS WACKY WITCH!
TIME I PUT MY FOOT DOWN... ON YOU!
BOOMMF
OR MAYBE NOT!
SPLOOSH
SPLOOSH
HANG IN THERE, RANGERS!
WE'LL THINK OF SOME-THING!
AT THIS POINT, THE BEST WAY TO HELP THEM MAY BE TO KEEP HER DISTRACTED!
AT LEAST UNTIL I CAN FIGURE OUT SOMETHING ELSE!
UH... TELL ME MORE... RITA...

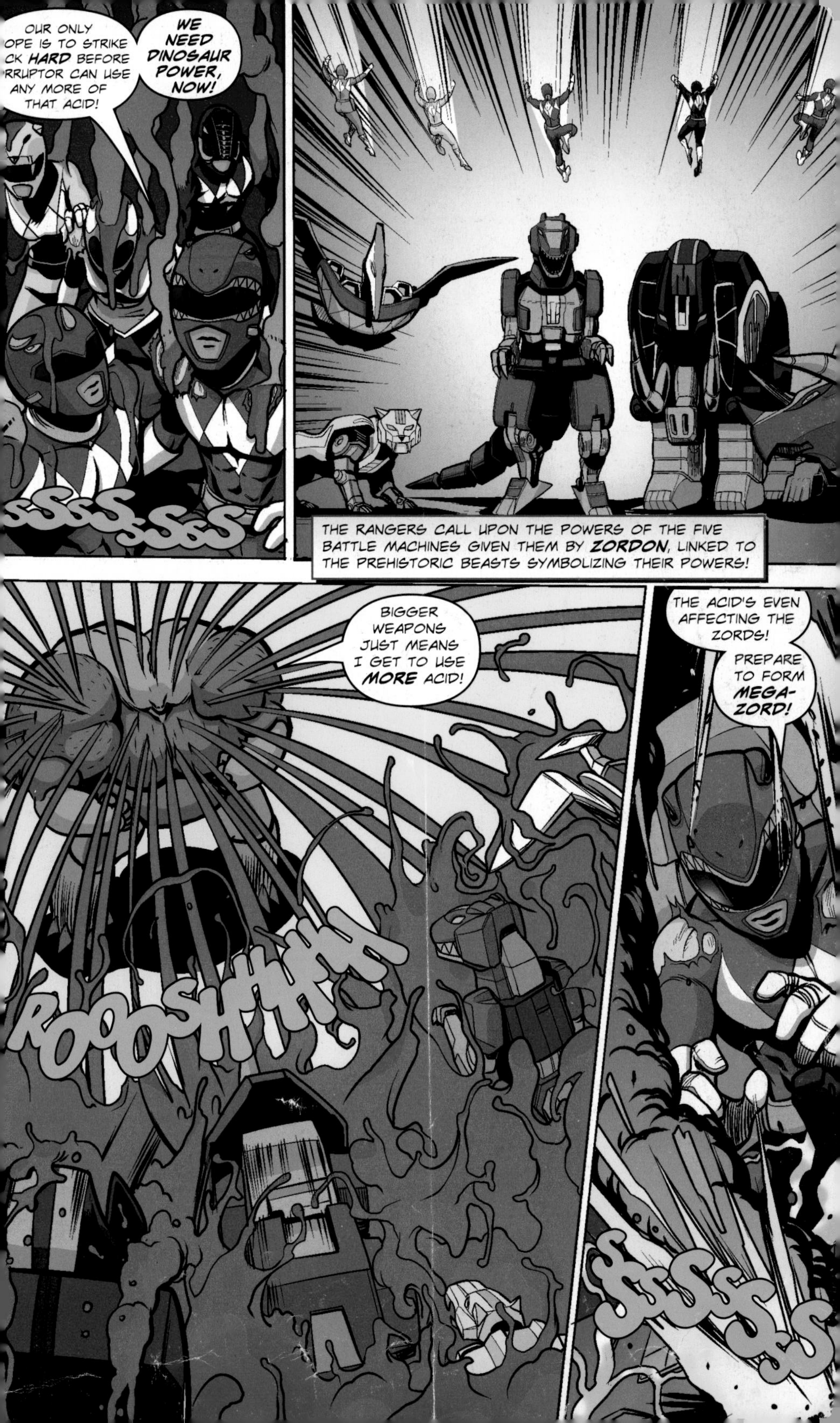
OUR ONLY
OPE IS TO STRIKE
CK HARD BEFORE
RRUPTOR CAN USE
ANY MORE OF
THAT ACID!
WE NEED DINOSAUR POWER, NOW!
SSSSSSS
THE RANGERS CALL UPON THE POWERS OF THE FIVE BATTLE MACHINES GIVEN THEM BY ZORDON, LINKED TO THE PREHISTORIC BEASTS SYMBOLIZING THEIR POWERS!
BIGGER WEAPONS JUST MEANS I GET TO USE MORE ACID!
ROOOSHHH
THE ACID'S EVEN AFFECTING THE ZORDS!
PREPARE TO FORM MEGA-ZORD!
SSSSSS

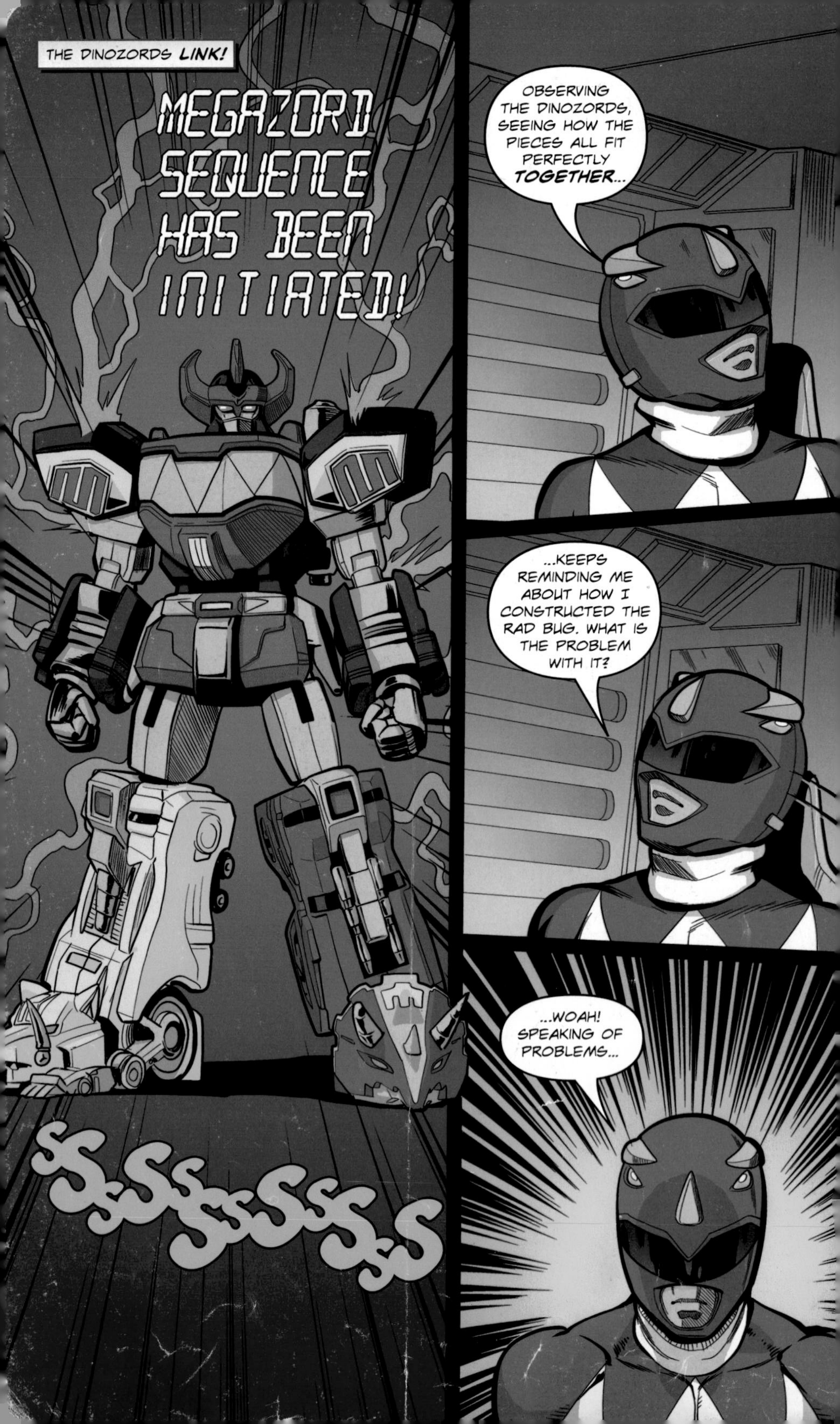
THE DINOZORDS LINK!
MEGAZORD SEQUENCE HAS BEEN INITIATED!
SSSSSSSSSS
OBSERVING THE DINOZORDS, SEEING HOW THE PIECES ALL FIT PERFECTLY TOGETHER...
...KEEPS REMINDING ME ABOUT HOW I CONSTRUCTED THE RAD BUG. WHAT IS THE PROBLEM WITH IT?
...WOAH! SPEAKING OF PROBLEMS...

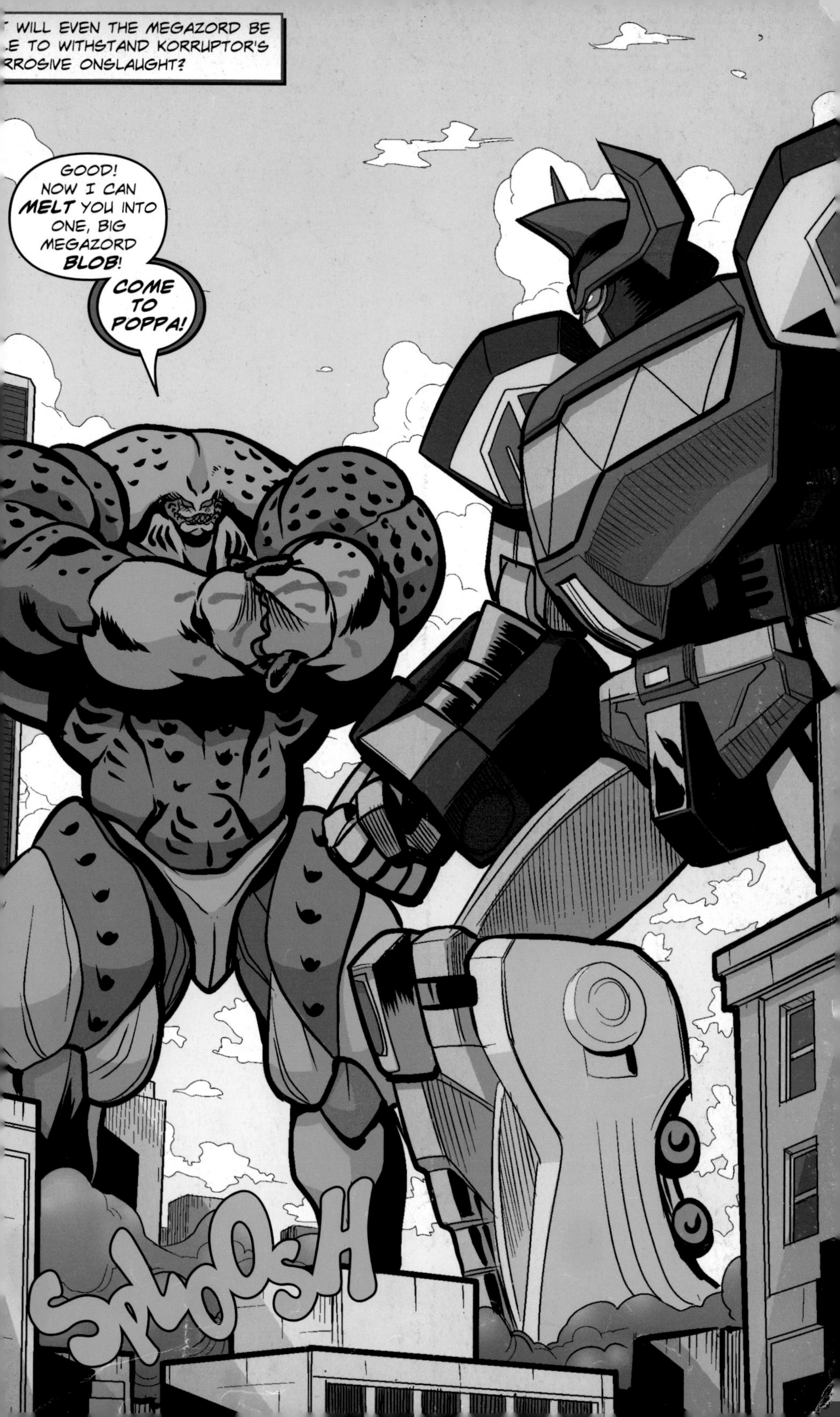

...T WILL EVEN THE MEGAZORD BE ...E TO WITHSTAND KORRUPTOR'S ...RROSIVE ONSLAUGHT?
GOOD! NOW I CAN MELT YOU INTO ONE, BIG MEGAZORD BLOB!
COME TO POPPA!
SPLOOSH

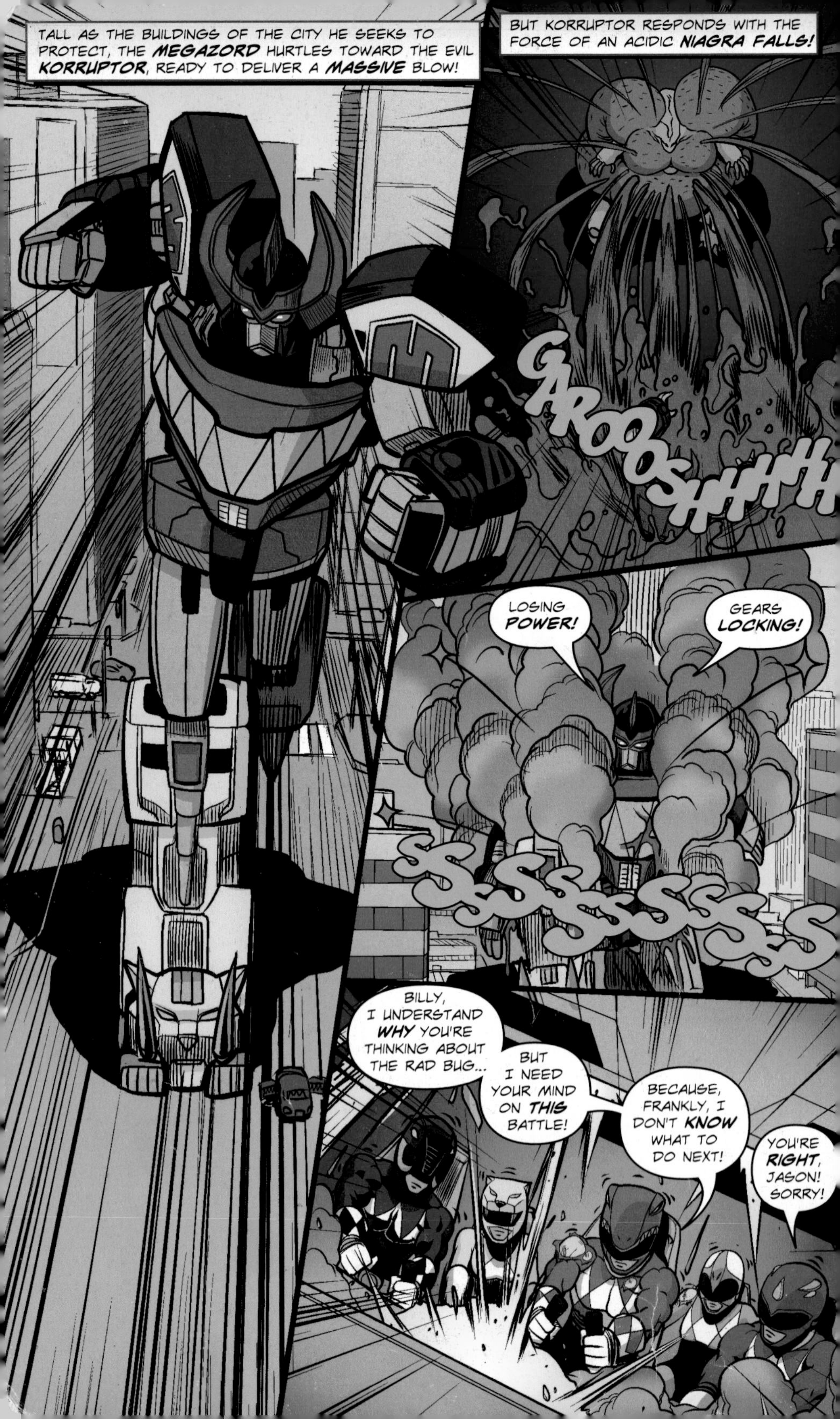
TALL AS THE BUILDINGS OF THE CITY HE SEEKS TO PROTECT, THE MEGAZORD HURTLES TOWARD THE EVIL KORRUPTOR, READY TO DELIVER A MASSIVE BLOW!
BUT KORRUPTOR RESPONDS WITH THE FORCE OF AN ACIDIC NIAGRA FALLS!
GAROOOSHHHH
LOSING POWER!
GEARS LOCKING!
SSSSSSSSSSS
BILLY, I UNDERSTAND WHY YOU'RE THINKING ABOUT THE RAD BUG...
BUT I NEED YOUR MIND ON THIS BATTLE!
BECAUSE, FRANKLY, I DON'T KNOW WHAT TO DO NEXT!
YOU'RE RIGHT, JASON! SORRY!

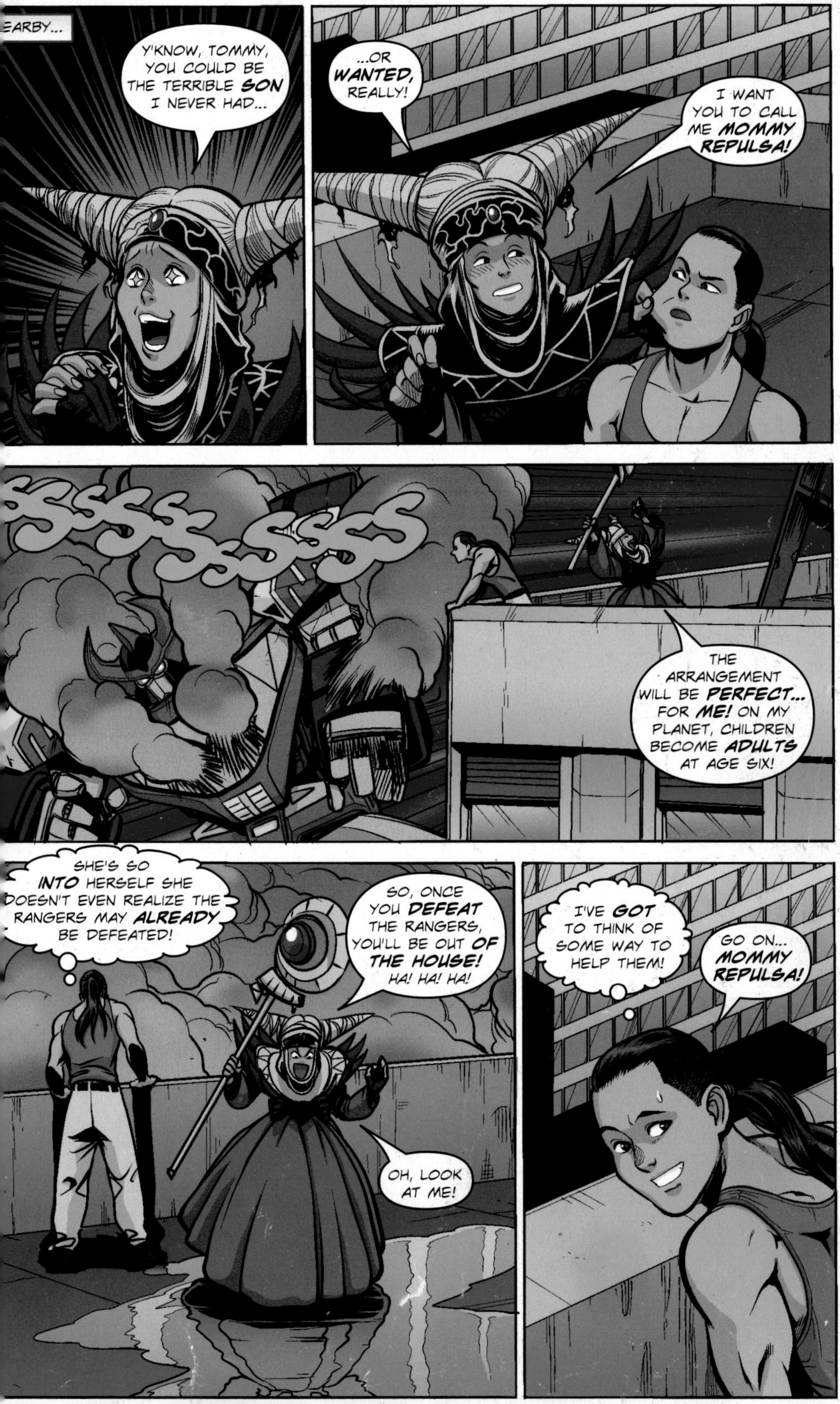

EARBY...
Y'KNOW, TOMMY, YOU COULD BE THE TERRIBLE SON I NEVER HAD...
...OR WANTED, REALLY!
I WANT YOU TO CALL ME MOMMY REPULSA!
SSSSSSSSSS
THE ARRANGEMENT WILL BE PERFECT... FOR ME! ON MY PLANET, CHILDREN BECOME ADULTS AT AGE SIX!
SHE'S SO INTO HERSELF SHE DOESN'T EVEN REALIZE THE RANGERS MAY ALREADY BE DEFEATED!
SO, ONCE YOU DEFEAT THE RANGERS, YOU'LL BE OUT OF THE HOUSE! HA! HA! HA!
OH, LOOK AT ME!
I'VE GOT TO THINK OF SOME WAY TO HELP THEM!
GO ON... MOMMY REPULSA!

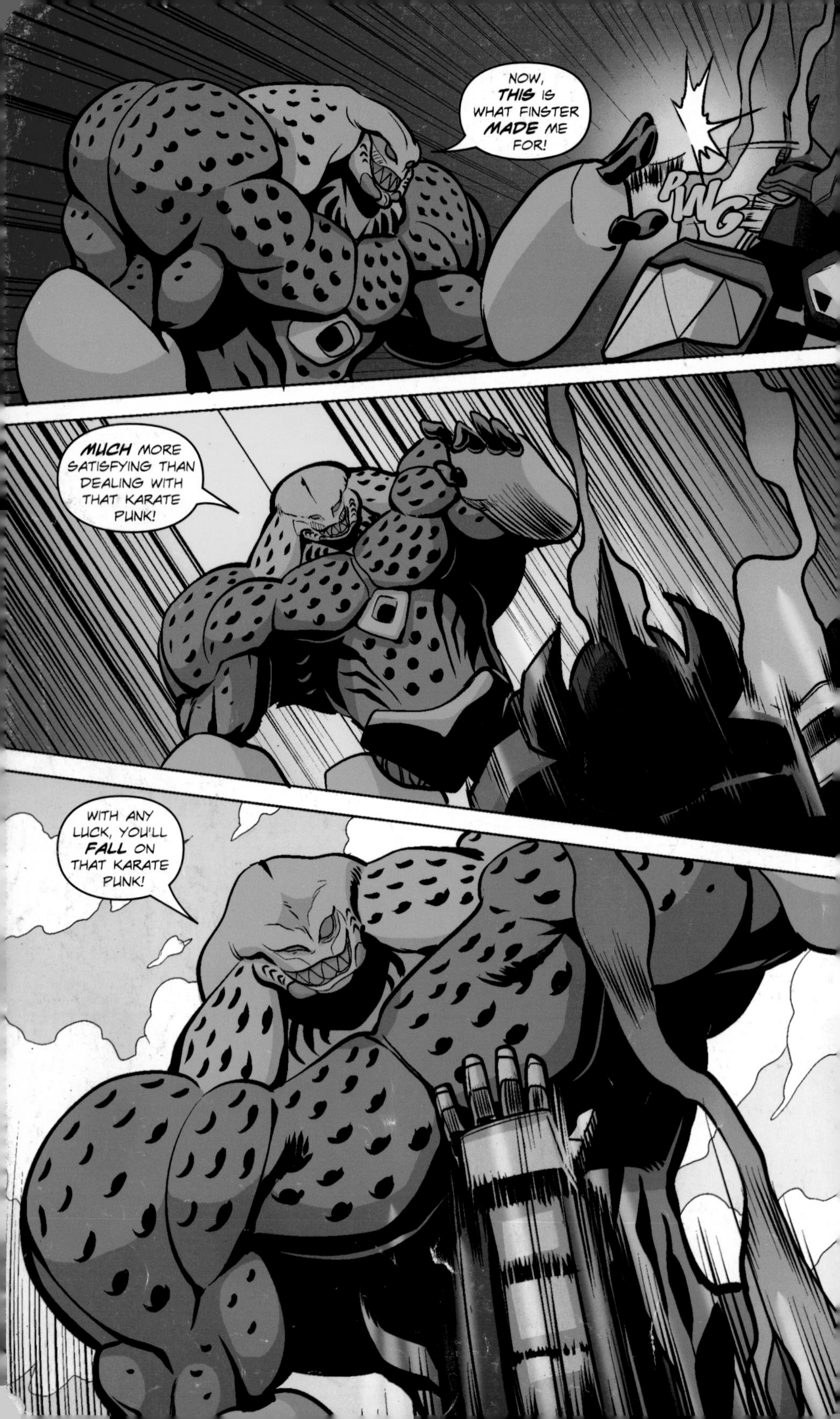
NOW, THIS IS WHAT FINSTER MADE ME FOR!
PING
MUCH MORE SATISFYING THAN DEALING WITH THAT KARATE PUNK!
WITH ANY LUCK, YOU'LL FALL ON THAT KARATE PUNK!

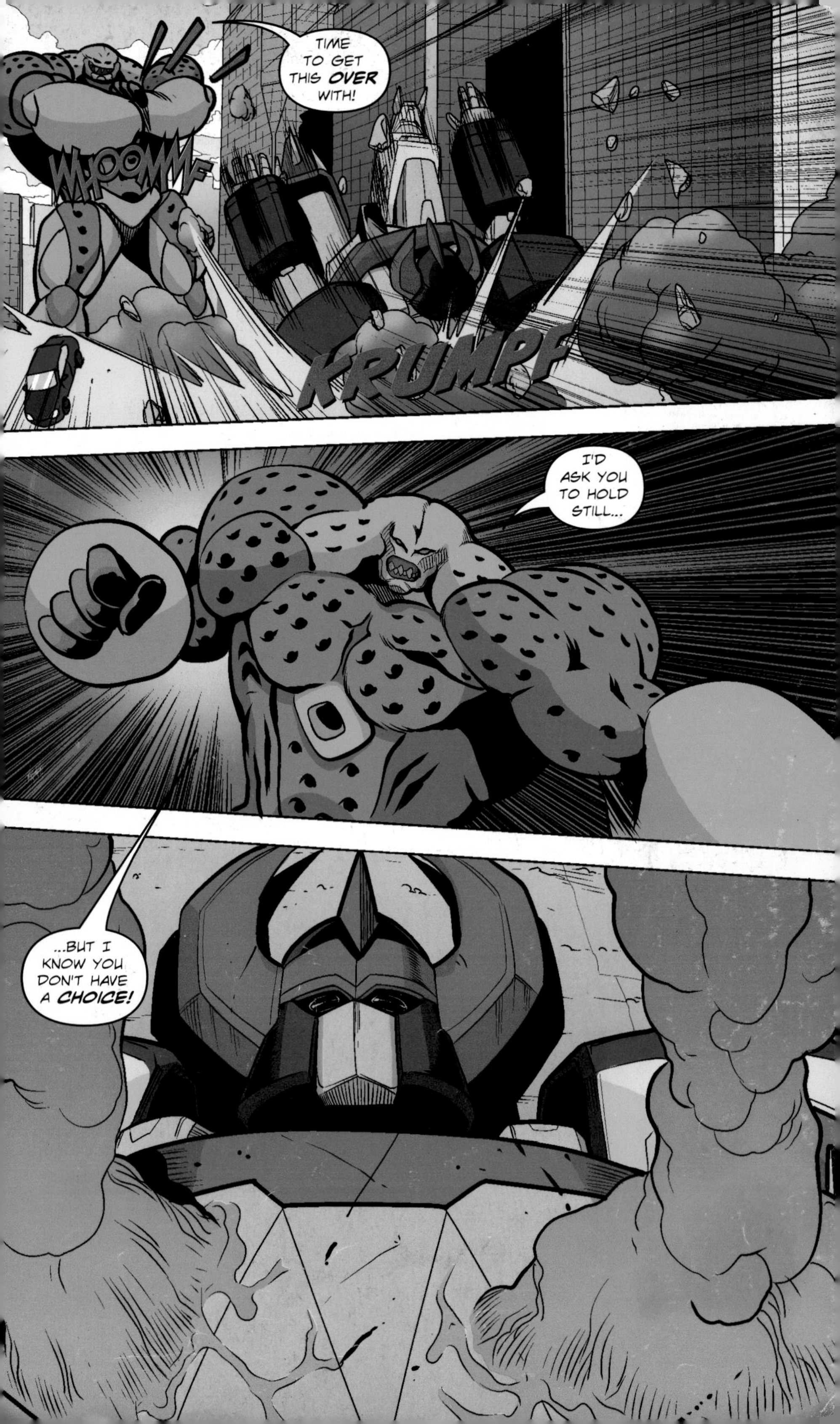
TIME TO GET THIS OVER WITH!
WHOOMMF
KRUMPF
I'D ASK YOU TO HOLD STILL...
...BUT I KNOW YOU DON'T HAVE A CHOICE!

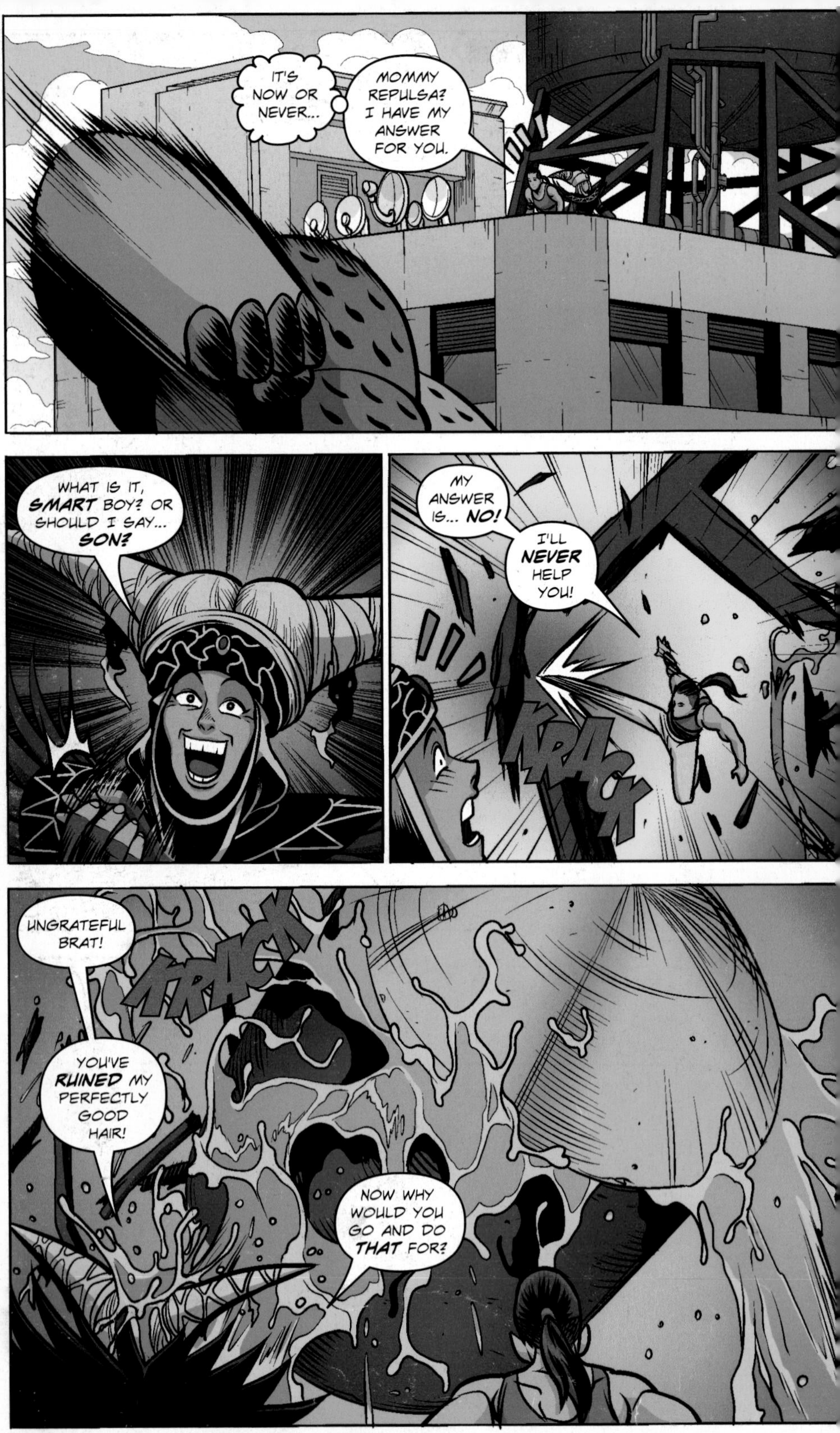
IT'S NOW OR NEVER...
MOMMY REPULSA? I HAVE MY ANSWER FOR YOU.
WHAT IS IT, **SMART** BOY? OR SHOULD I SAY... **SON?**
MY ANSWER IS... **NO!**
I'LL **NEVER** HELP YOU!
KRACK
UNGRATEFUL BRAT!
KRACK
YOU'VE **RUINED** MY PERFECTLY GOOD HAIR!
NOW WHY WOULD YOU GO AND DO **THAT** FOR?

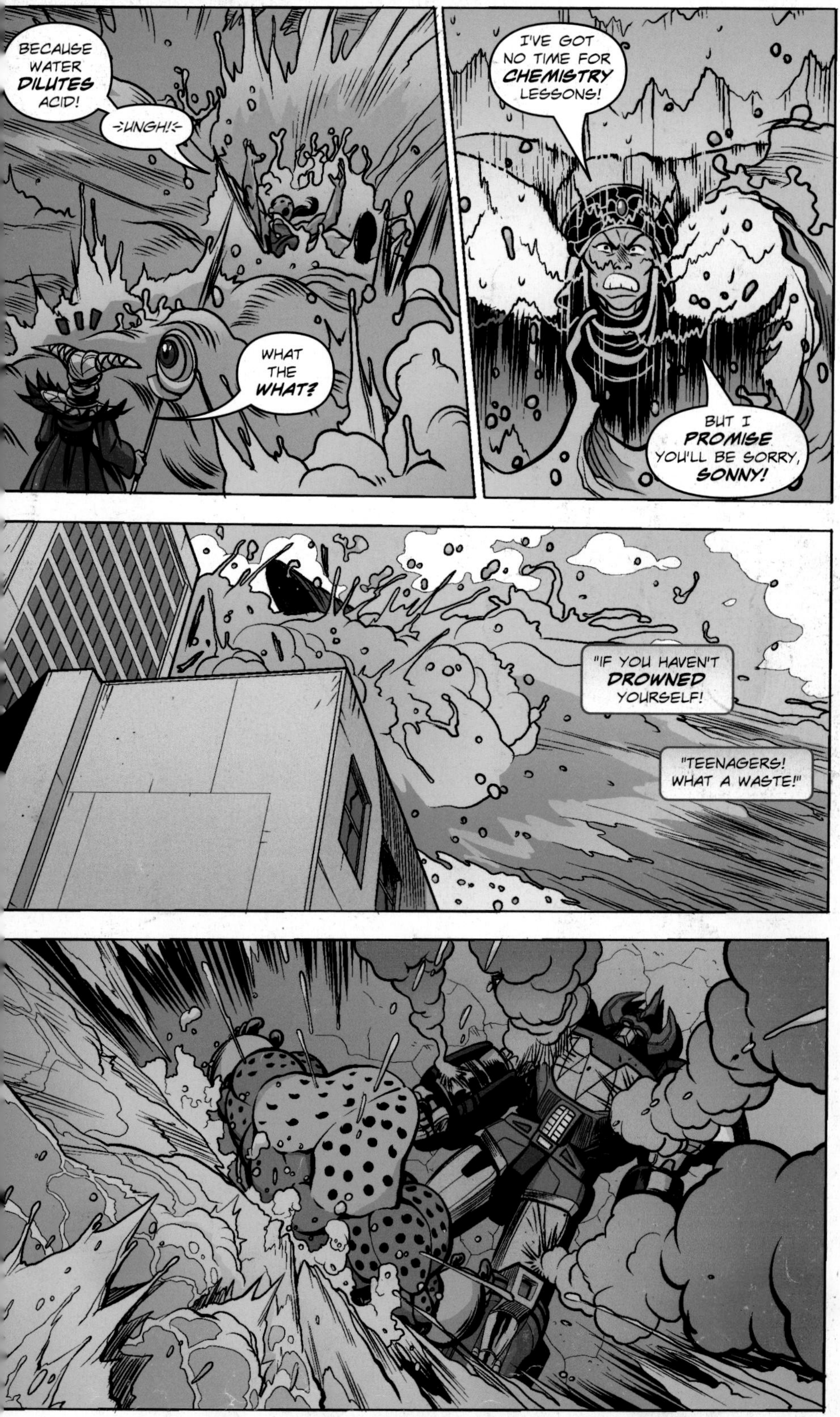
BECAUSE WATER DILUTES ACID!
-UNGH!-
WHAT THE WHAT?
I'VE GOT NO TIME FOR CHEMISTRY LESSONS!
BUT I PROMISE YOU'LL BE SORRY, SONNY!
"IF YOU HAVEN'T DROWNED YOURSELF!
"TEENAGERS! WHAT A WASTE!"

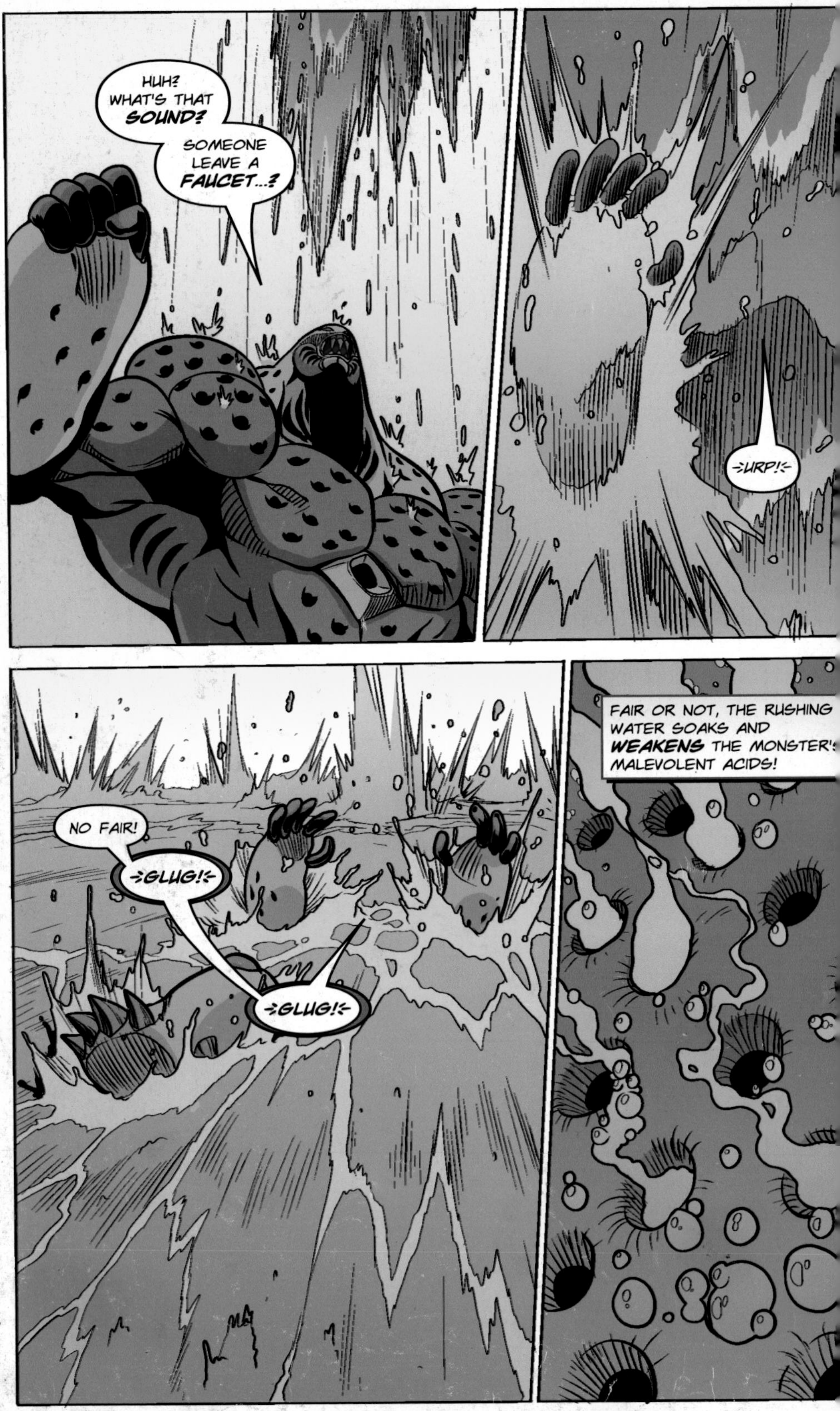
HUH? WHAT'S THAT SOUND?
SOMEONE LEAVE A FAUCET...?
URP!
NO FAIR!
GLUG!
GLUG!
FAIR OR NOT, THE RUSHING WATER SOAKS AND WEAKENS THE MONSTER'S MALEVOLENT ACIDS!

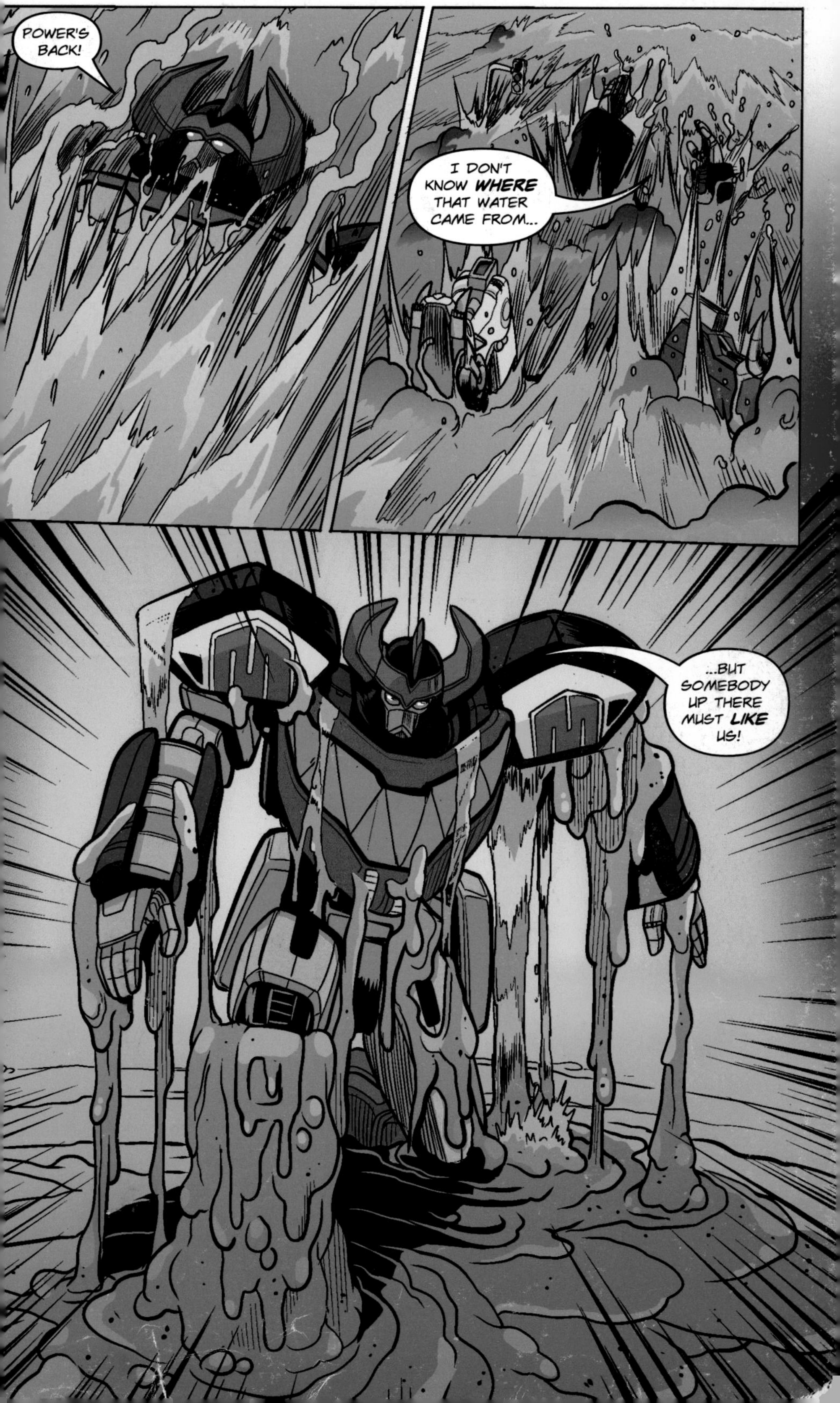
POWER'S BACK!
I DON'T KNOW WHERE THAT WATER CAME FROM...
...BUT SOMEBODY UP THERE MUST LIKE US!

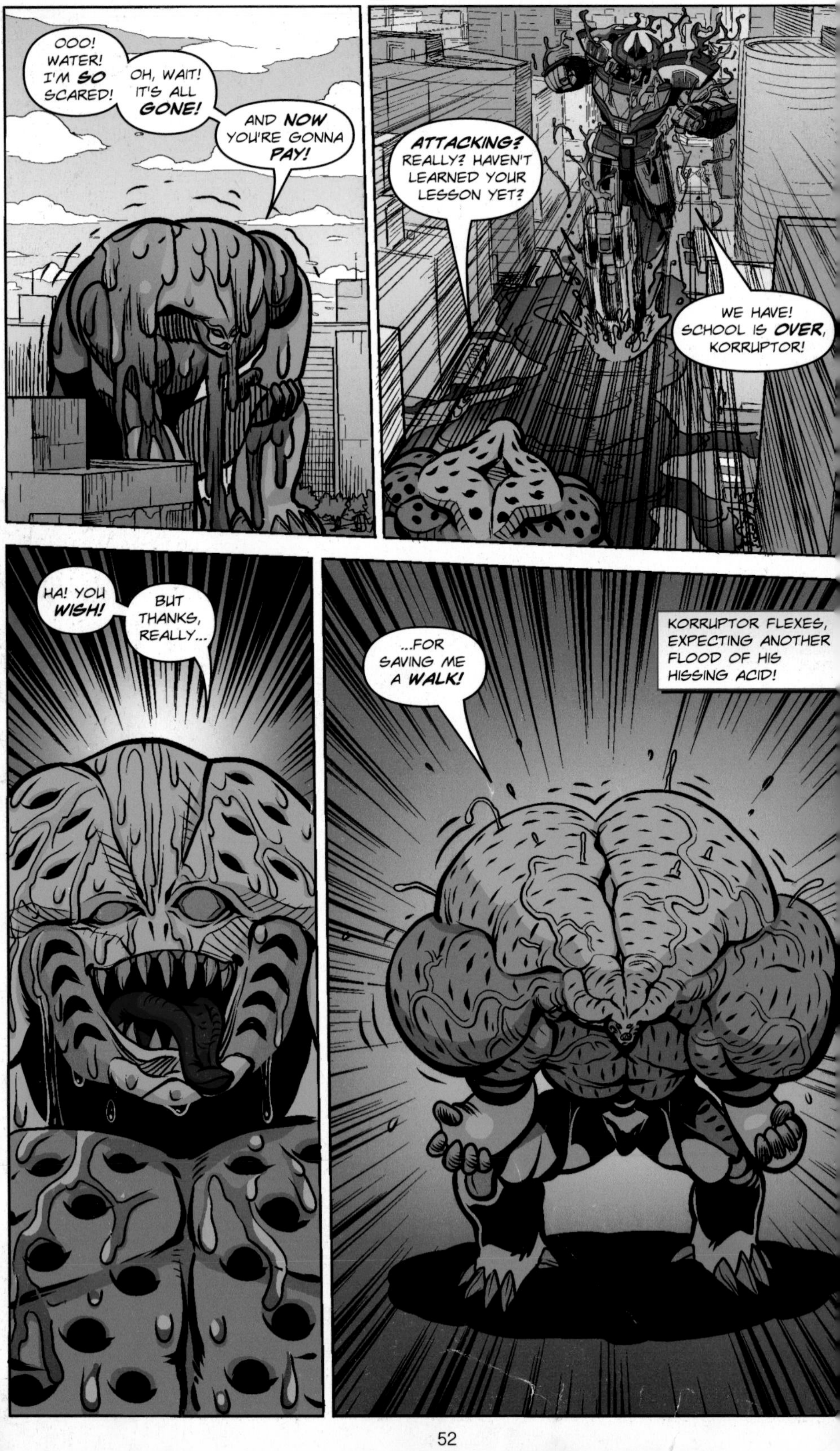
OOO! WATER! I'M **SO** SCARED!
OH, WAIT! IT'S ALL **GONE!**
AND **NOW** YOU'RE GONNA **PAY!**
**ATTACKING?** REALLY? HAVEN'T LEARNED YOUR LESSON YET?
WE HAVE! SCHOOL IS **OVER**, KORRUPTOR!
HA! YOU **WISH!**
BUT THANKS, REALLY...
...FOR SAVING ME A **WALK!**
KORRUPTOR FLEXES, EXPECTING ANOTHER FLOOD OF HIS HISSING ACID!

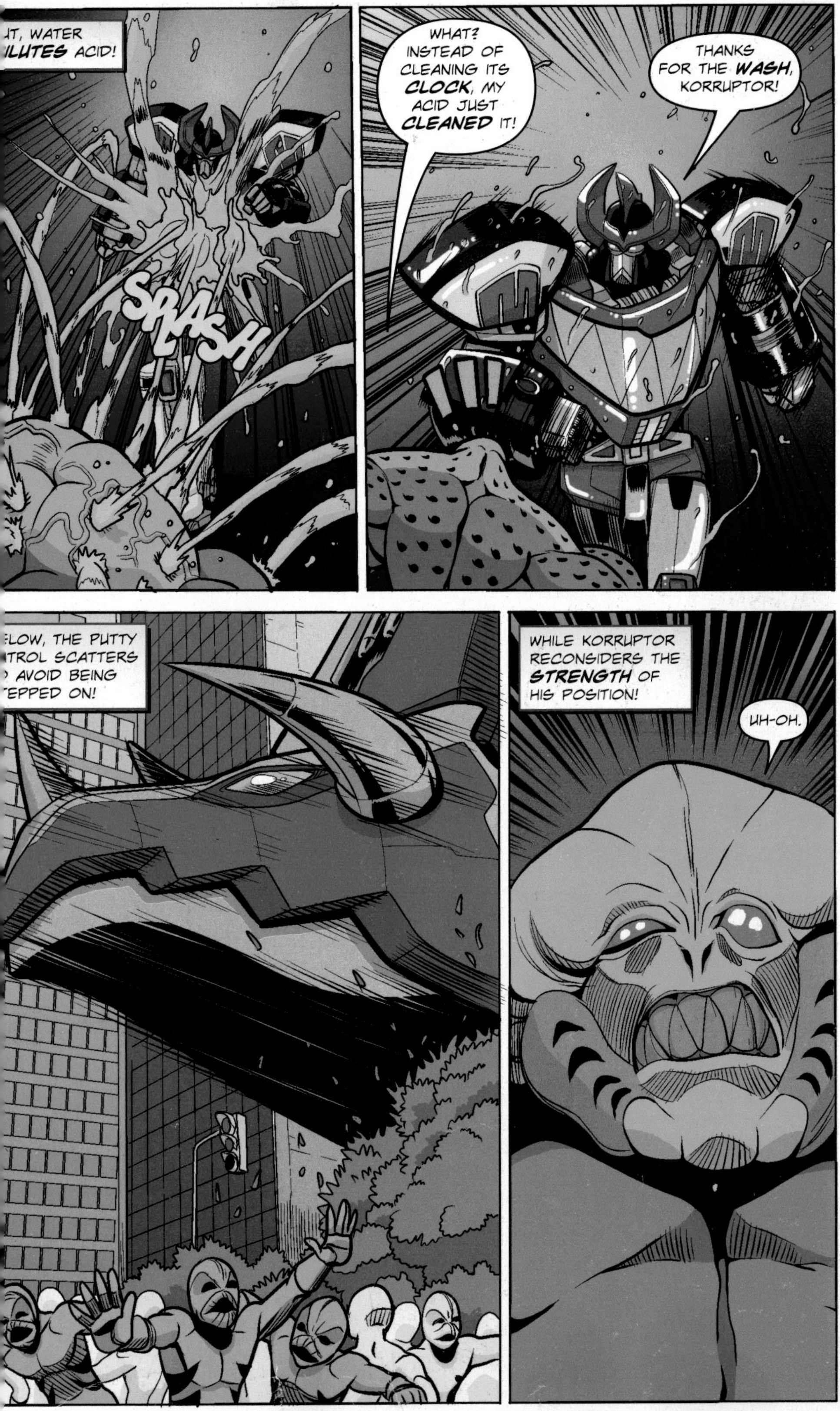
IT, WATER
DILUTES ACID!
SPLASH
WHAT? INSTEAD OF CLEANING ITS CLOCK, MY ACID JUST CLEANED IT!
THANKS FOR THE WASH, KORRUPTOR!
ELOW, THE PUTTY
TROL SCATTERS
AVOID BEING
TEPPED ON!
WHILE KORRUPTOR RECONSIDERS THE STRENGTH OF HIS POSITION!
UH-OH.

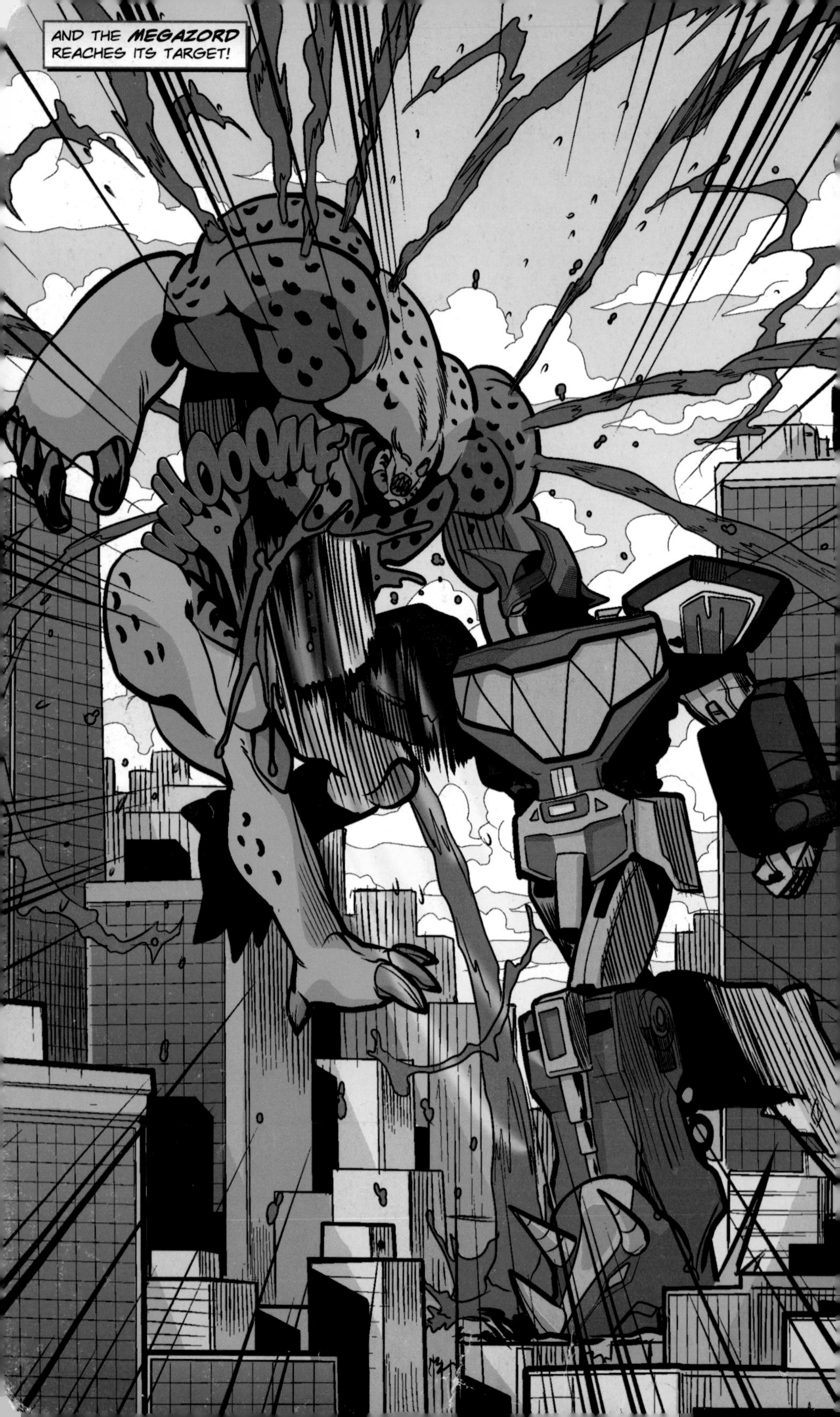
AND THE MEGAZORD REACHES ITS TARGET!
WHOOOMF

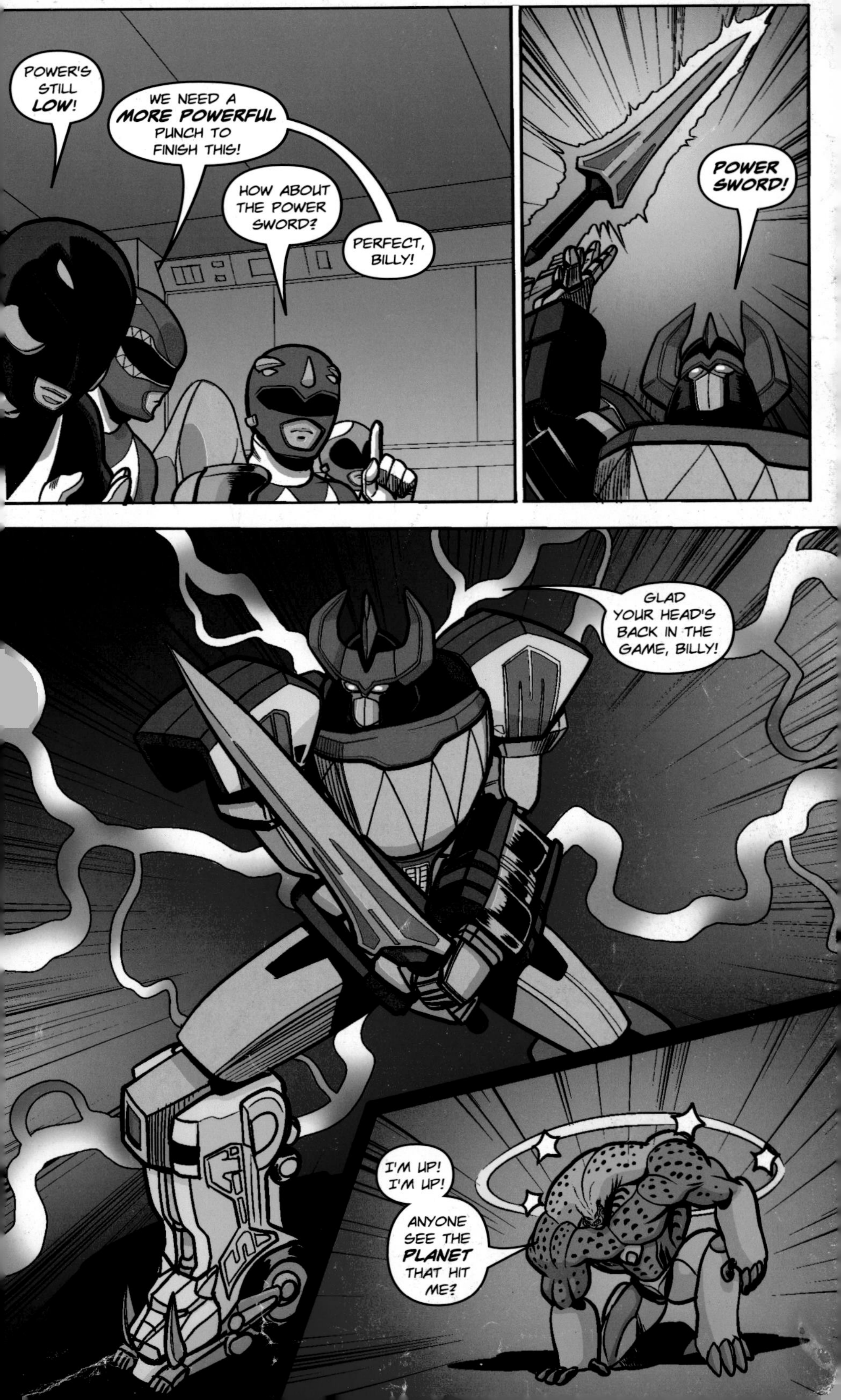
POWER'S STILL LOW!
WE NEED A MORE POWERFUL PUNCH TO FINISH THIS!
HOW ABOUT THE POWER SWORD?
PERFECT, BILLY!
POWER SWORD!
GLAD YOUR HEAD'S BACK IN THE GAME, BILLY!
I'M UP! I'M UP!
ANYONE SEE THE PLANET THAT HIT ME?

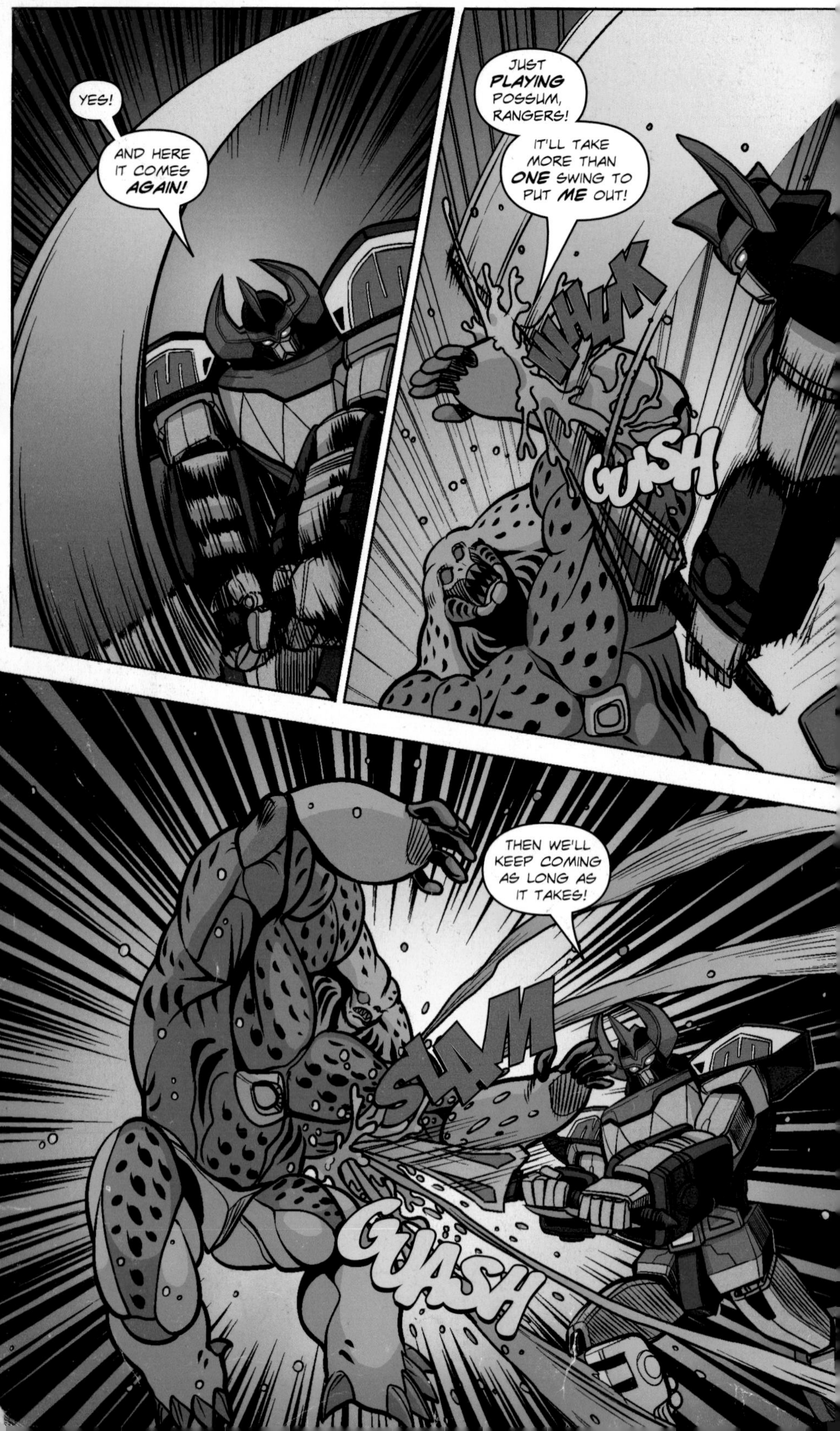
YES!
AND HERE IT COMES AGAIN!
JUST PLAYING POSSUM, RANGERS!
IT'LL TAKE MORE THAN ONE SWING TO PUT ME OUT!
WHUK
GUSH
THEN WE'LL KEEP COMING AS LONG AS IT TAKES!
SLAM
GUASH

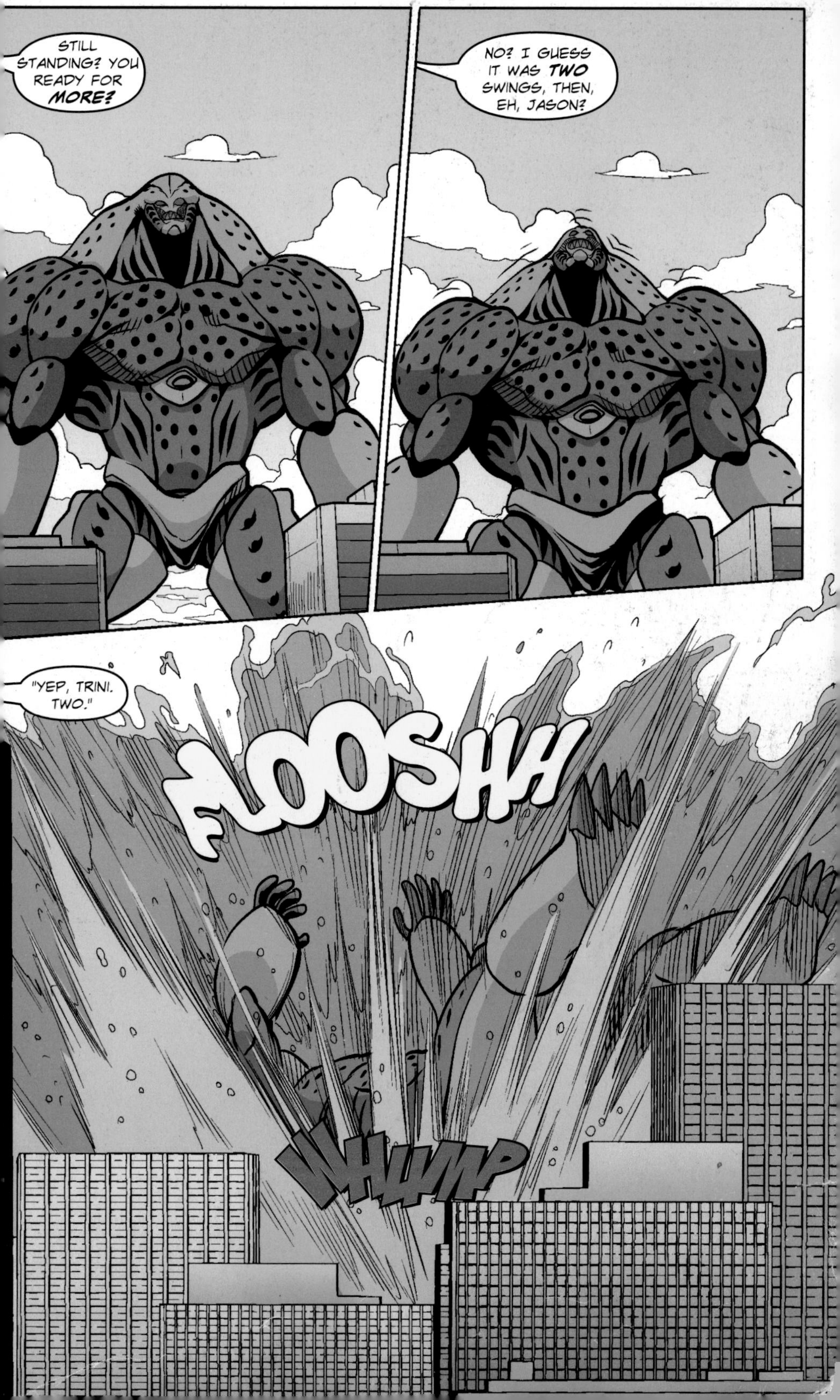
STILL STANDING? YOU READY FOR MORE?
NO? I GUESS IT WAS TWO SWINGS, THEN, EH, JASON?
"YEP, TRINI. TWO."
FLOOSHH
WHUMP

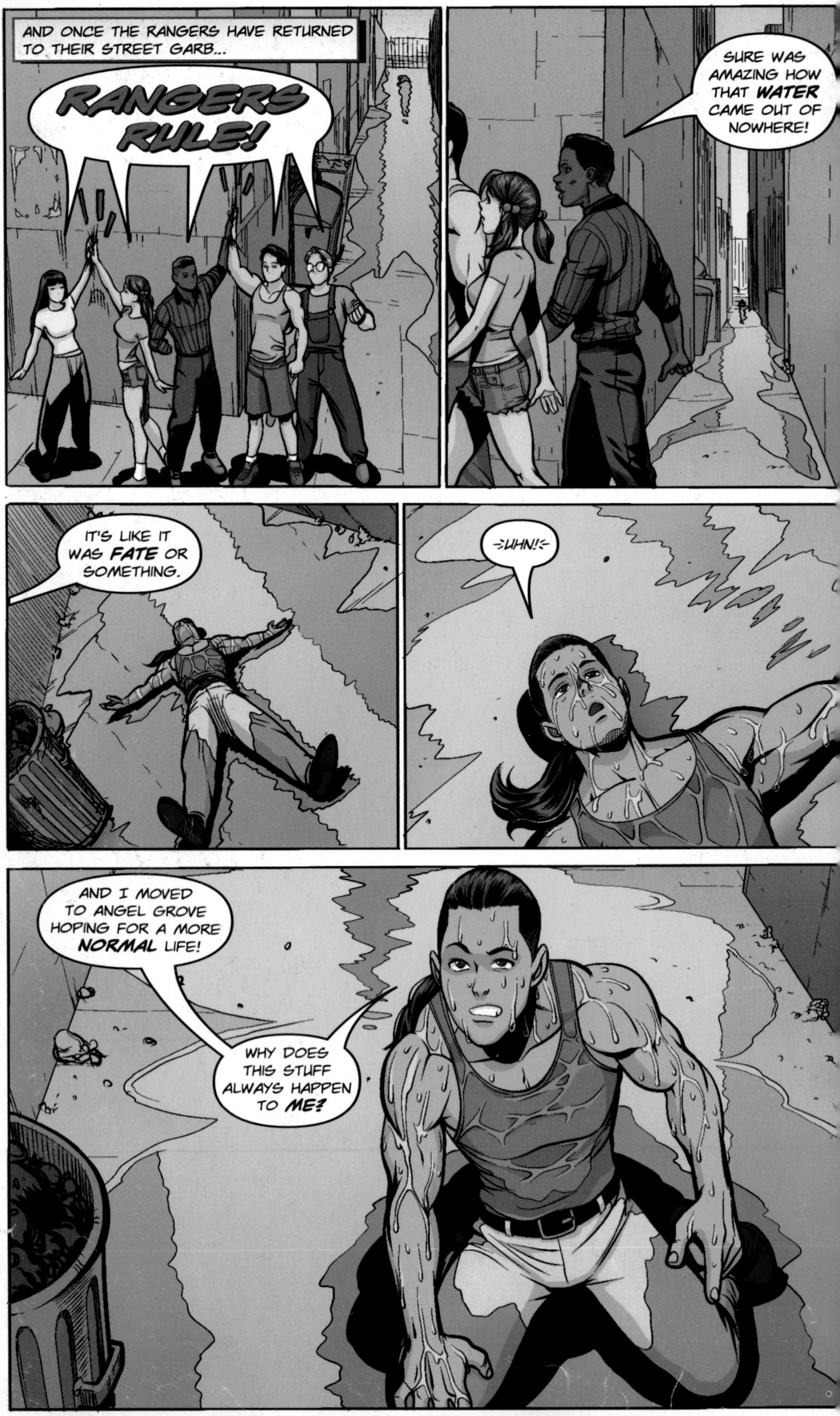
AND ONCE THE RANGERS HAVE RETURNED TO THEIR STREET GARB...
RANGERS RULE!
SURE WAS AMAZING HOW THAT WATER CAME OUT OF NOWHERE!
IT'S LIKE IT WAS FATE OR SOMETHING.
UHN!
AND I MOVED TO ANGEL GROVE HOPING FOR A MORE NORMAL LIFE!
WHY DOES THIS STUFF ALWAYS HAPPEN TO ME?

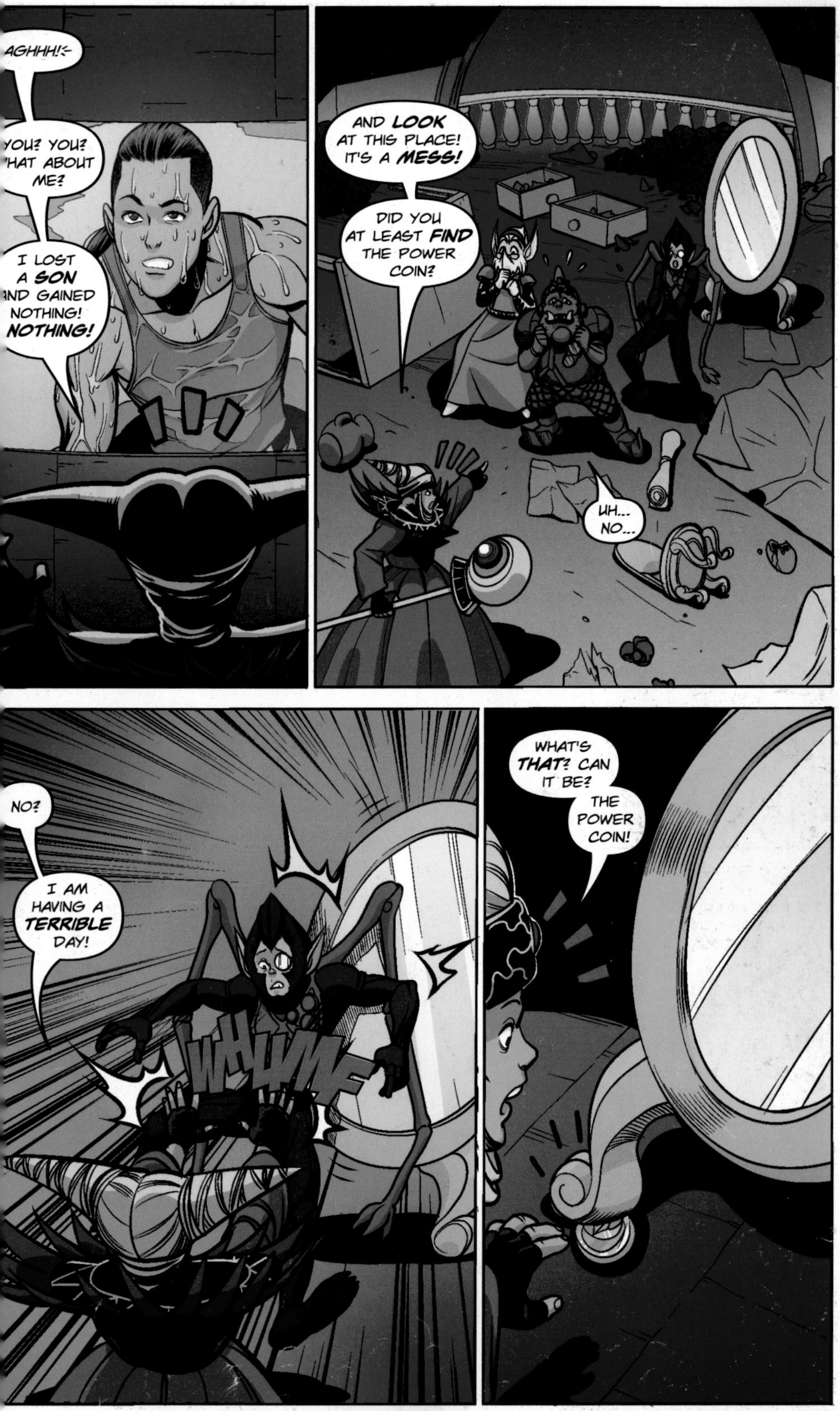
AGHHH!!
YOU? YOU? WHAT ABOUT ME?
I LOST A SON AND GAINED NOTHING! NOTHING!
AND LOOK AT THIS PLACE! IT'S A MESS!
DID YOU AT LEAST FIND THE POWER COIN?
UH... NO...
NO?
I AM HAVING A TERRIBLE DAY!
WHUMF
WHAT'S THAT? CAN IT BE?
THE POWER COIN!

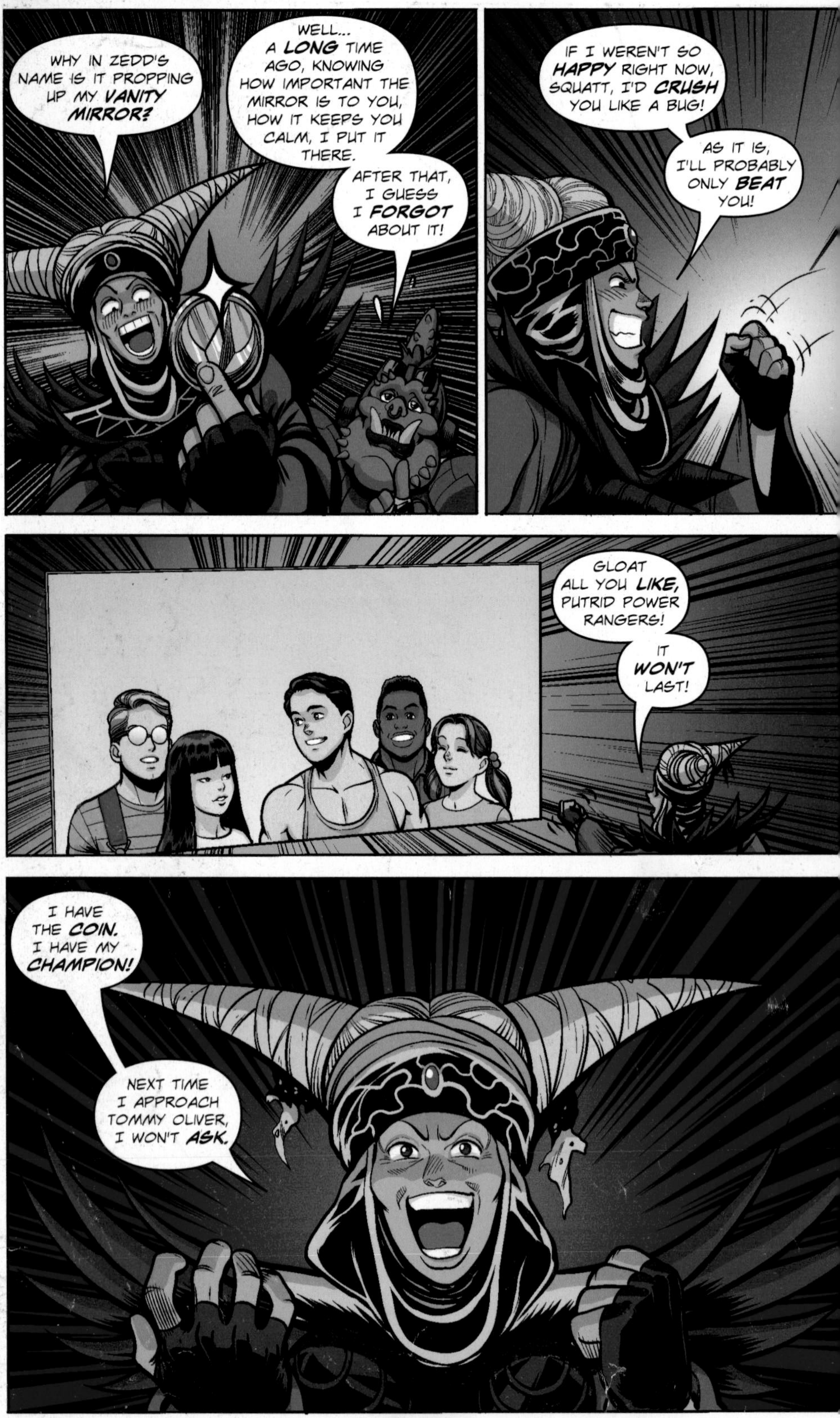
WHY IN ZEDD'S NAME IS IT PROPPING UP MY VANITY MIRROR?
WELL... A LONG TIME AGO, KNOWING HOW IMPORTANT THE MIRROR IS TO YOU, HOW IT KEEPS YOU CALM, I PUT IT THERE.
AFTER THAT, I GUESS I FORGOT ABOUT IT!
IF I WEREN'T SO HAPPY RIGHT NOW, SQUATT, I'D CRUSH YOU LIKE A BUG!
AS IT IS, I'LL PROBABLY ONLY BEAT YOU!
GLOAT ALL YOU LIKE, PUTRID POWER RANGERS!
IT WON'T LAST!
I HAVE THE COIN. I HAVE MY CHAMPION!
NEXT TIME I APPROACH TOMMY OLIVER, I WON'T ASK.

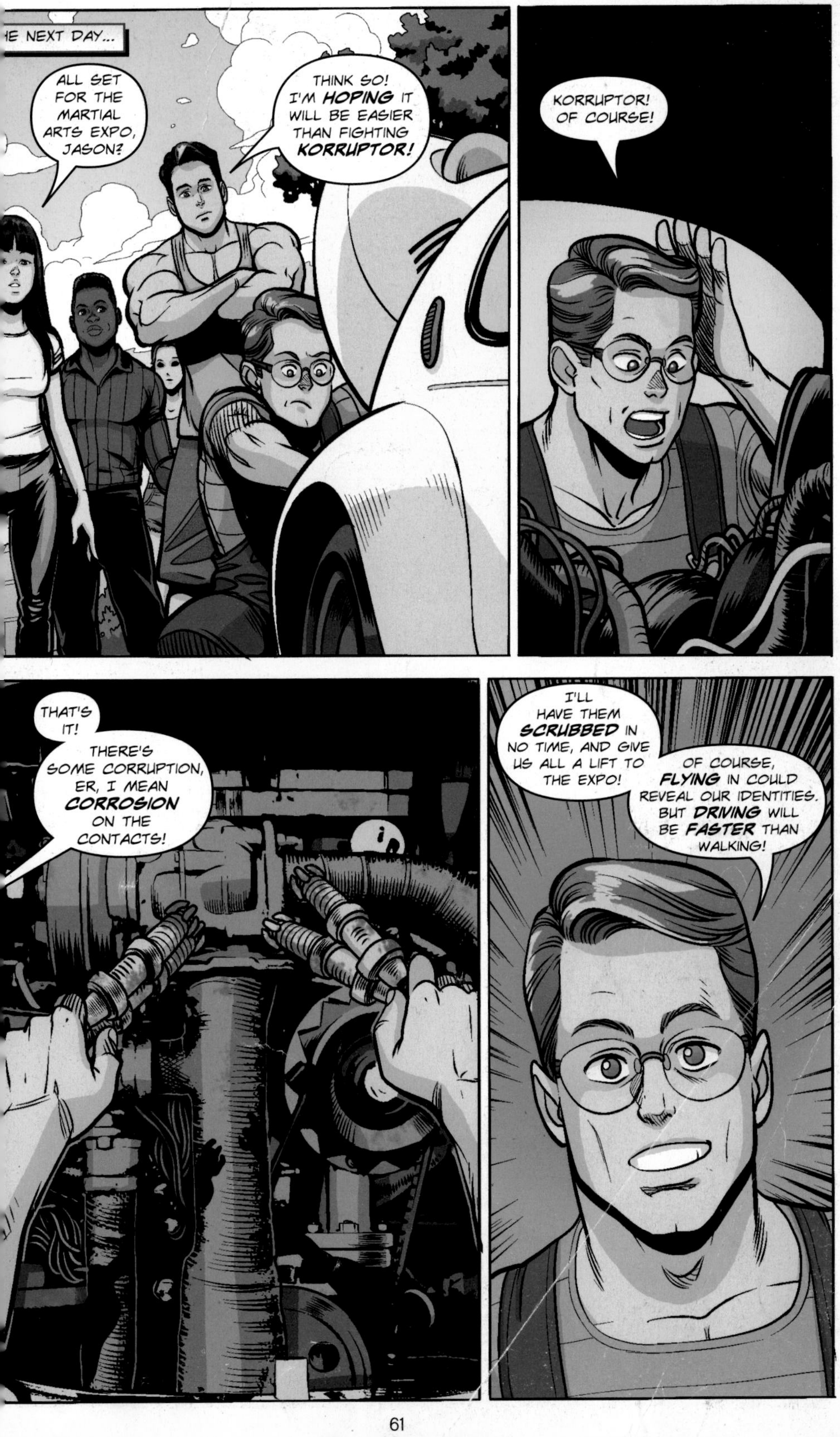
HE NEXT DAY...
ALL SET FOR THE MARTIAL ARTS EXPO, JASON?
THINK SO! I'M HOPING IT WILL BE EASIER THAN FIGHTING KORRUPTOR!
KORRUPTOR! OF COURSE!
THAT'S IT!
THERE'S SOME CORRUPTION, ER, I MEAN CORROSION ON THE CONTACTS!
I'LL HAVE THEM SCRUBBED IN NO TIME, AND GIVE US ALL A LIFT TO THE EXPO!
OF COURSE, FLYING IN COULD REVEAL OUR IDENTITIES. BUT DRIVING WILL BE FASTER THAN WALKING!

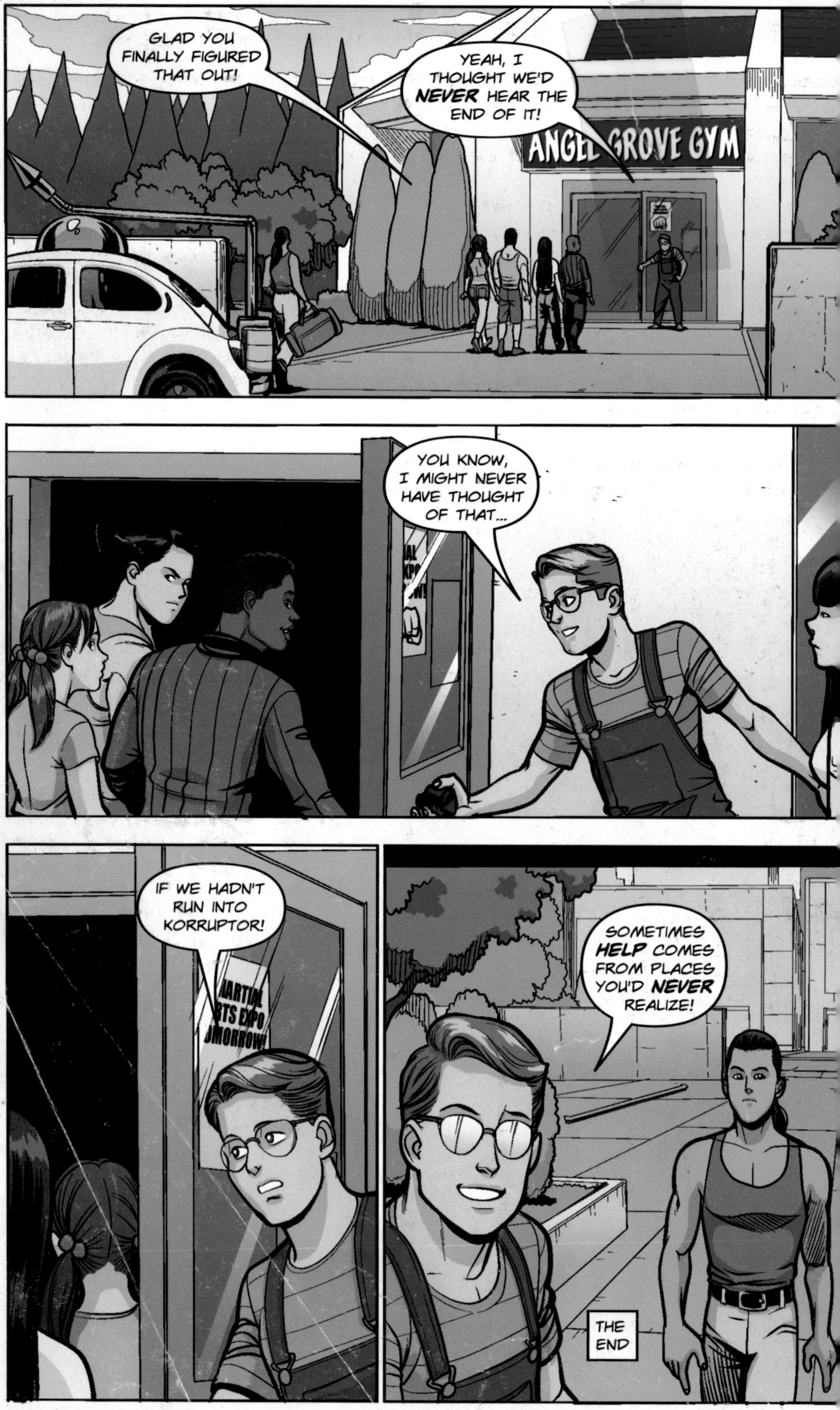
GLAD YOU FINALLY FIGURED THAT OUT!
YEAH, I THOUGHT WE'D **NEVER** HEAR THE END OF IT!
ANGEL GROVE GYM
YOU KNOW, I MIGHT NEVER HAVE THOUGHT OF THAT...
IF WE HADN'T RUN INTO KORRUPTOR!
SOMETIMES **HELP** COMES FROM PLACES YOU'D **NEVER** REALIZE!
THE END

# WATCH OUT FOR PAPERCUTZ™

lcome to the super-powered second MIGHTY MORPHIN POWER RANGERS graphic novel, by Stefan rucha and PH Marcondes, from Papercutz, the slightly amorphous comics company dedicated to lishing great graphic novels for all ages. I'm Jim Salicrup, the Editor-in-Chief, AKA the Prematurely y Ranger, and I'm here with all sorts of thrilling announcements and behind-the-scenes fun…

haps the biggest, most exciting news for any MIGHTY MORPHIN POWER RANGERS fan was recently nounced in *Variety*, and other Hollywood trade news magazines—coming July 22, 2016, at a theater r you—an all-new POWER RANGERS motion picture! Saban Brands and Lionsgate have announced berto Orci as executive producer for the first original live action Power Rangers feature film. Orci will elop the story along with writers Ashley Miller and Zach Stentz. Orci's writing credits include *The azing Spider-Man 2, Star Trek, Transformers* and *Mission: Impossible III*. Miller and Stentz have previously tten screenplays for *X-Men: First Class* and *Thor*. That's got to be the biggest news regarding MMPR ce Papercutz announced last year at the San Diego Comic-Con that we'd be publishing MIGHTY RPHIN POWER RANGERS graphic novels!

t don't for one second think we've run out of surprises! Take this very graphic novel, for example. en writer Stefan Petrucha suggested that he'd bring on a special co-writer, I was curious who he had in mind. He told me that it was a celebrity who was a big fan of the Power Rangers—but that can be so many people! Finally he revealed it was **Ryan Buell**, co-creator and host of TV's *Paranormal State*. Stefan had previously worked with Ryan co-writing *Paranormal State: My Journey into the Unknown* and even appearing on a couple of episodes of *Paranormal State* the TV series (I've always known Stefan was interested in such things, which is why he was the perfect choice to write THE X-FILES comics back in the early 90s.). We can't tell you how thrilled we were to have Ryan contribute to this very special story and hope you enjoy it as much as we do!

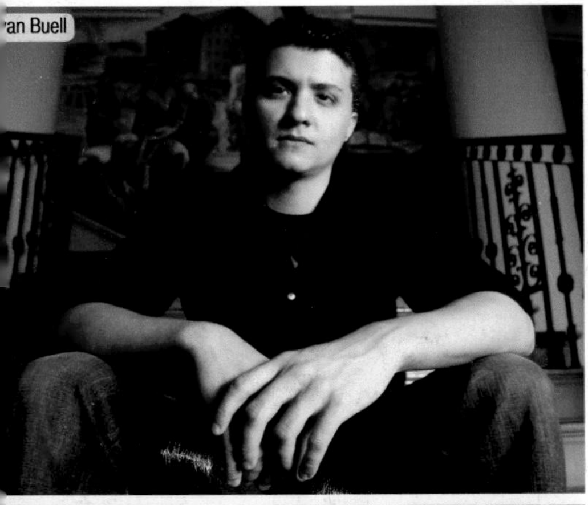
an Buell

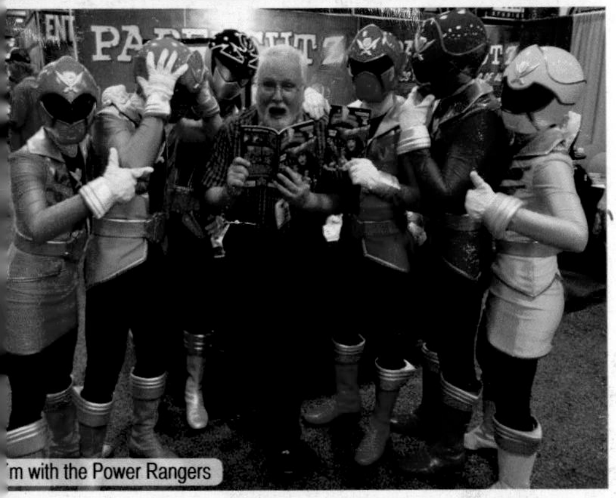
m with the Power Rangers

But the best is yet to come! In MIGHTY MORPHIN POWER RANGERS #3 "By Bug, Betrayed!" we'll be featuring two big stories starring The Mighty Morphin Power Rangers, plus a report from the 2014 Power Morphicon from Editor Michael Petranek. Trust me, you don't want to miss this one! If nothing else, it'll give you something to do while waiting for a certain movie to premiere on July 22, 2016!

Go, go, POWER RANGERS!

Thanks,

Jim


**STAY IN TOUCH!**

EMAIL: salicrup@papercutz.com
WEB: papercutz.com
TWITTER: @papercutzgn
FACEBOOK: PAPERCUTZGRAPHICNOVELS
SNAIL MAIL: Papercutz, 160 Broadway, Suite 700, East Wing, New York, NY 10038

THE MIGHTY MORPHIN POWER RANGERS WILL RETURN IN "BY BUG, BETRAYED!"

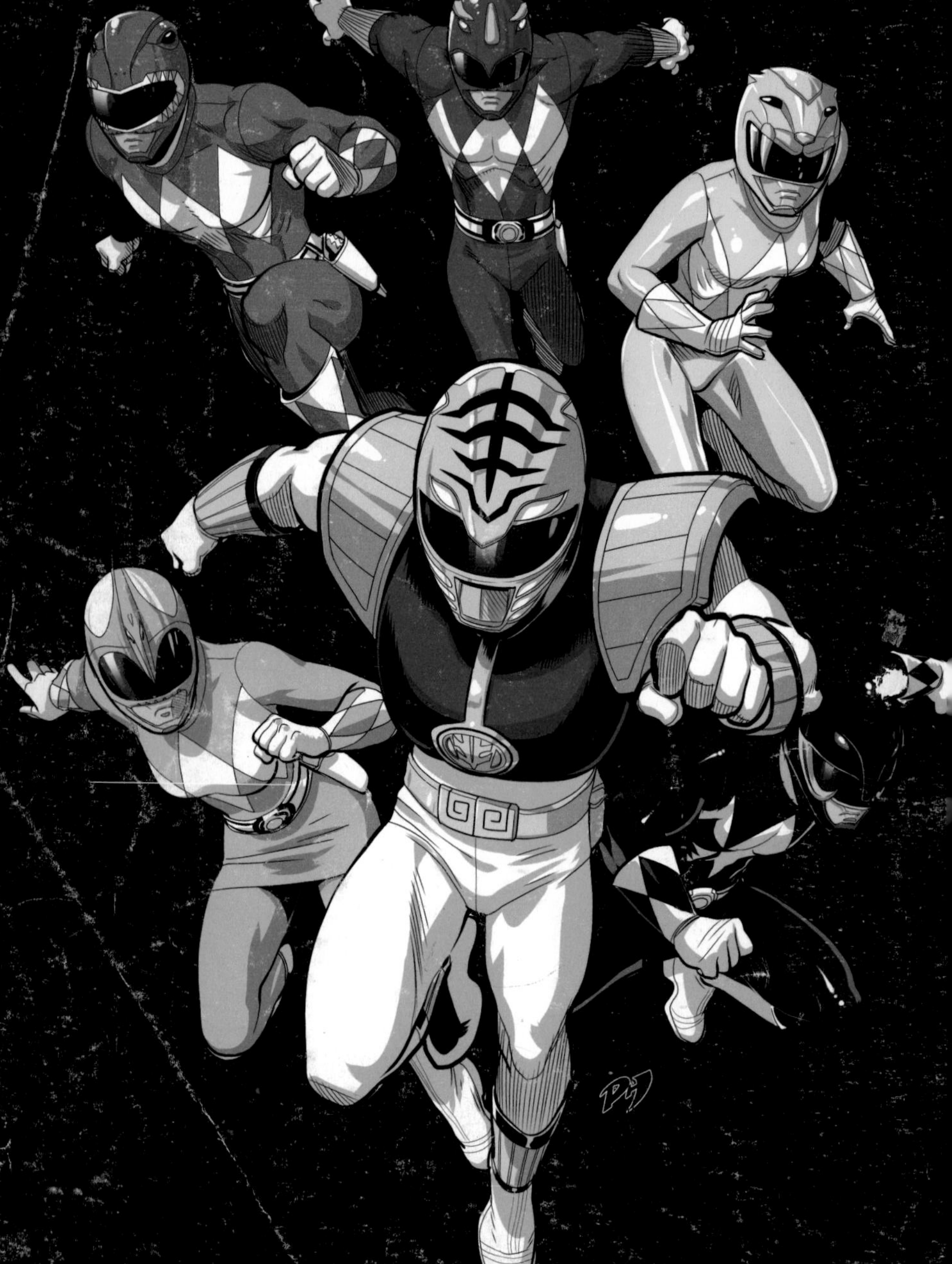

COMING SOON!